Boomi's Boombox

SHANTHI SEKARAN

BOOMi's BOOMBOX

KATHERINE TEGEN BOOKS
An Imprint of HarperCollins Publishers

Katherine Tegen Books is an imprint of HarperCollins Publishers.

Library of Congress Control Number: 2022052145
ISBN 978-0-06-305158-4

Typography by Laura Mock
23 24 25 26 27 LBC 5 4 3 2 1
First Edition

For Avi and Ash

TRACK 1
Another One Bites the Dust

There's something you should know about the summer. It's a time for dreamers and time wasters, for half-baked ideas and unfinished songs. It's a blink of a season. There's never enough of it. One day it's spring and the next it's autumn, but for a shimmering moment in the middle, summer steps into your life, your sudden best friend, taking your hand, babbling in your ear, showing you her secrets, promising to stay forever.

But spring? Spring was another story. That spring, the only things babbling were the teachers on my laptop. All day, all week, all year long. I'd spent the entire sixth grade sitting at our kitchen table, staring at this screen, my classmates boxed into tidy computerized rectangles. It was the second spring of the pandemic. Covid-19 had been sprinting around the world for a whole year, and it showed no signs of slowing.

Before Covid, when I actually went to school, I was a person. A walking, talking, hand-raising, lunch-eating, test-taking person. On a computer screen, I was just a box with a face. I was nobody. I was nowhere. I spent most days gazing out of our living room window at the branches of a eucalyptus tree, as cars hummed by on the street and my grandmother's game shows tinned from the television. Every now and then, I'd hear a spray of melody from my mom's office, where she taught cello lessons online. I'd watch the gray morning sky turn to afternoon blue, then back to gray as the fog rolled in.

Just wait for summer, I'd tell myself. *Everything's better in the summer.* And was it? Maybe. It was stranger, that's for sure. More impossible than anything I might have dreamed up those spring afternoons.

Let's hit fast-forward. Or is it rewind? My impossible summer started one weekend in July, at tryouts for the Academie Fontaine, where I'd been a ballet student my whole life. I was twelve, and twelve-year-olds had to try out if they wanted to graduate to the Studio Company, the highest level of the academy. I'd been a ballet dancer since I was little, really little. My mom told me that before I could walk, she'd hold my hands above my head and help me glide along the floor on my tiptoes. I loved ballet from the second I saw Olga Petrov leap and spin across a computer screen. I was six years old, sitting on the sofa with Mom. Olga was playing Clara from *The Nutcracker,* dressed in a long violet nightgown. She jumped and landed like a whisper, like she barely weighed an ounce.

But let's get back to my story. The year was 2021. That's me, Boomi Gopalan, age twelve, second from stage left. You've probably noticed my white tights with smudges on the knees, the black leotard, and the little paunch of a belly still hanging over my legs. The other girls—including my best friend, Bebe Jacobs—were dressed in white tights and black leotards, too, but they seemed to have lost their paunches.

I hadn't seen Bebe in person for over a year. Her face had changed. Her hair had grown, and now she wore it in a bun, like a real ballerina. Mom had tried to wind my hair into a bun, but it kept spinning out like a crazy pinwheel. She eventually gave up and tied it in a ponytail, which sagged lazily down my back now.

In the front row sat Madame Fontaine, a clipboard bouncing on her lap as she jiggled one knee. Scattered through the rows behind her: the parents. They'd come to watch us for this final phase of auditions, our last chance to prove to Madame Fontaine that we belonged in the Studio Company, that we really and truly were *company dancers*, not little goofballs in tutus. Ten of us would be chosen, and the chosen would train five times a week. If I made it, my life would become dance and dance would become my life. If I didn't make it, well—I didn't want to think about that.

The stage lights cast a ghostly glow over the rows of seats, and I could see Bebe's mom tugging nervously at her mask. I could see my mom, her yellow scarf tied around her hair, gripping herself by the neck. The parents, all in masks, stared at us like we were juggling knives, like we were holding *their* lives in the perfect curves of our arabesques. And there I was, teetering into the spotlight, on my pointe shoes—those are

3

the shoes you see ballet dancers perform in, the kind that let you dance right up on your toes, like some kind of superhuman. I wasn't too confident on pointe. My tiptoes weren't my happy place, I guess. I was really more of a flat-on-my-feet person, more of a not-falling-over person. I hated pointe shoes so much that I tried to ditch them that morning.

In the car, when Mom checked my bag and found the shoes missing, she was not amused. "What is your exact problem with pointe shoes?" she snapped. My exact problem with pointe shoes was that they hurt. But I didn't bother telling Mom that. She wouldn't understand.

Madame's secretary moved down the audition list, calling out names. Bebe went before me. She was perfect. She danced like she was born on pointe. She seemed not to even notice the three grand jetés we had to do. She leaped and landed like she'd done those big, arcing jumps every day of her life. I could have watched her dance all day.

But then: "Boomi D. Gopalan!" the secretary called.

Normally, when I dance, the rest of the world falls away. I couldn't tell you who I was, what I had for breakfast, or what homework was due the next day. Dance was an animal that lived inside me, and when I let it loose, it took me over. Each time I did a turn, the animal lifted my heels for me, it thrust my arms, it snapped my head around in perfect sync.

But during my audition that day, my mind kept getting in the way. I started to remember things that had nothing to do with dance. One second, I was glissading across the stage.

And the next, I saw Dad's jacket hanging on the kitchen chair, just where he'd left it the day he got sick.

One second, I was doing a grand jeté—

And the next, I saw Dad in a hospital bed, a tube sticking out from his mouth—

Soaring through the air in a saut de chat—

Then at a funeral home, holding my mom's hand—

Then I was back onstage for the final steps of the piece, the bourree en couru. When you really nail it, you look like a swan skimming across a lake, the movements of your feet so tiny and precise that they hardly seem to move at all. I lifted onto my toes, but just as I took that first step, I thought again of that tube going into Dad's mouth. My feet forgot what to do. My ankles buckled. My arms swung in big frantic circles as I tried to regain my balance. Finally, my legs gave way. I spilled like a pile of rocks onto the hard wood surface of the stage. And then I just sat there on my butt, blinking out at the dim rows of seats, at my mom, whose hands had moved to her cheeks, who sat there with her eyes closed, like she was trying to be anywhere but in that auditorium. And just like that, my ballet days were over.

TRACK 2
Walls Come Tumbling Down!

An hour later, Madame's secretary stepped out of the office, holding a sheet of paper that listed the ten chosen academy dancers. She walked in rapid steps down the hallway, pinching the list between her thumb and forefinger and holding it at a distance, like it smelled bad. Then she pinned the list to the bulletin board, took one look at the mob approaching, and hightailed it out of there. "Six feet apart!" someone's mom kept yelling. No one listened. Students and parents crowded around the list, jostling to get a good look. Squeals and whoops erupted from the dancers who'd made it.

I searched for my name, Boomika Devi Gopalan. A little spark of hope fizzed in my chest as my eyes moved through the names. Sure, I'd crash-landed onstage, but at least I'd stood out! Different could be good, sometimes. Right?

Right?

Wrong. Ten names. Bebe Jacobs was one of them. Boomika Devi Gopalan was not. Of course I didn't make it. The group scattered, some of us chattering happily, some of us in tears. Some of us were dancers still. The rest of us—well, I guess the rest of us just weren't.

That's when I felt my mom tugging at my wrist, leading me down the long hallway, away from the exit.

"We're going the wrong way!" I warned her.

"Oh no we're not." Next thing I knew her knuckles were rapping on Madame Fontaine's office door. My heart pounded. My throat went dry. The door opened—it wasn't the secretary. It was Madame herself.

She teetered over us like an ancient tree, her big, round glasses balanced on the tip of her nose. Mom has an English accent, and usually the second she opens her mouth, people fall a little bit in love with her. But Madame Fontaine had a French accent, so I guess she wasn't impressed by Mom's English one. She gazed down, bored and impatient as Mom prattled on. I don't really know *what* Mom was even saying, because I was focused on Madame's glasses. Every few seconds, they slid down her nose, and Madame pushed them back up again.

I could hear Mom's voice tremble, like she was about to cry. I knew she wasn't faking it. I wondered if she'd actually break into sobs, but like Madame Fontaine's glasses, she held on. She said what she had to say. And Madame's answer, in her prim French accent? I remember it word for word: "Boomi is a very good dancer. Very good. But she is big." My cheeks flamed up. My insides twisted and tangled. The lady didn't miss a beat, just said it straight out. *She eez BEEG.* And she didn't stop there. "In this academy," she said, "we look for a certain . . . shape of the body. This becomes very important, in my experience, as dancers progress—"

"If Boomi lost the weight, would you reconsider?" Mom's question rang through the empty hallway.

Madame Fontaine said nothing. Her eyes flitted from my face to my legs and back again. Then she disappeared into her office and came back with a file folder. She looked through it for a few seconds.

"Well," she said. "Her barre and center work were just fine. But more important, Boomi is incapable of dancing on pointe."

Madame Fontaine had a point. (Ha, ha.) We all saw me fall. The fact of my fall walked up and stood there, right next to me, hairy and ridiculous, like Bigfoot in a tutu.

Madame Fontaine pursed her lips and gazed down at me. "Good day, then. Thank you for your time." She gave her glasses one last hearty shove and started to close the door.

"Wait!" Mom grabbed the door, stopped it from closing. I don't remember the rest very well, because I don't want to. I stood there and tried not to hear when Mom said *Her father* and *just last year* and *a hard time a second chance her weight issue pointe shoes.*

Madame Fontaine sniffed down at her folder and gazed at me for a few endless seconds. "I'll have to speak to the board," she said. "We do have a wonderful *modern* dance program. Open to all abilities. Children love it. Good day." She slammed the door shut. Mom stared at me, her eyelids drooping, her face sagging.

On the drive home, she was quiet, her silence filling the car. Lights reflected from the street slid across her face, her eyes barely blinking. She looks nothing like me. I'm sure she'd make a perfect ballerina. She's small and delicate, like a figurine in a music box.

"I'm sorry I screwed up," I said.

She didn't answer. Silently, we searched for parking, circling the neighborhood for an open spot, until, miraculously, we found one just outside our building. That almost *never* happens. Normally, Mom would say something like *Rock star parking!* and we'd high-five. But that didn't happen. She just parked, opened her door, and made her way up the stairs into our building.

Here's the thing. I am big. BEEG. Not just fat but tall. The nurse at my doctor's office called me *sturdy*. Bebe's mom called me *sporty*. Mom calls me *big boned*. That's the dumbest one of all. My bones had nothing to do with how fat I was. For most of my life, I'd never thought about being big or small. My body was just a thing I used. It helped me run and dance. It was super happy to eat whatever I gave it, as long as that wasn't zucchini. It didn't matter that I'd grown a head taller than Bebe, or that she and I looked so different in our leotards.

But when I turned eleven, things changed. I kept growing, kept getting taller, growing past my mom, catching up to my dad. But my body didn't stretch out like a piece of gum. Instead, it puffed up like a poori. Everything on me got softer and rounder and wider. At first, Mom said it was no big deal—this kind of thing just happened at my age. But it wasn't just my age that changed me. Something else happened that year. My dad died. He got Covid—*lots* of people got Covid that year—and lots of people got better. I always thought he'd get better, too. Instead, he got worse. And then he was gone.

More things changed after that. Mom changed. Our house changed—it got quieter and emptier, like *it* missed my dad, too. Shadows I'd never seen before started to creep out of the walls, perching in their corners, sliding across the sofa, waiting for Dad to come home.

And here's another thing that changed. I couldn't dance on pointe anymore. I'd been able to do it—I really had! But when Dad died, I lost my balance. I never got it back.

Even when I wasn't dancing, it got harder to move my body around, like someone had hung little weights on my bones. Was it sadness I was carrying? Can missing someone really change how you move? How you dance? Can it knock you off your pointe shoes and send you crashing to the stage?

From my seat in the car, I looked up and saw the clouds move, blown by the wind, gray and smoky against the dark sky. A moment later, the moon poked out, just a shy sliver of it. I'd give anything for a big fat full moon, for a moon with a friendly face on it, a moon with a cow jumping over it, a moon made of cheese—anything but the cold little blade that hung above me now. It was comforting to think that the moon, at least, would grow full again. But what about me?

TRACK 3
Our House

We live in a two-story Victorian duplex across the street from Golden Gate Park. Our duplex is a house that's split in two, lengthwise, with two front doors, two front windows, two little balconies, and two triangle-shaped roofs. Its two owners painted it two different colors, so our half of the house is blue and the other half is yellow. I stared at our two-story Victorian duplex for a very long time. Why? Because every molecule in my body wished it didn't have to go in.

When I finally got out of the car, I saw that I wasn't alone. Denny sat leaning against our building, wrapped in a gray coat that looked weirdly familiar. Denny was a man who spent most days on our sidewalk, sitting against our building, his giant rucksack at his side, his eyes closed, letting the sun bake his pink cheeks. He's been around for as long as I can remember. I used to find Dad down here with him some days, chatting or playing cards or just sitting and thinking. The night after Dad died, I stood staring out my window. I caught sight of Denny and he looked up at me, tears streaming down his face. Ever since that night, I've looked for Denny every night after dinner. And every night, he's been there. Usually, we just wave. It makes me feel better to know he's around.

Denny saluted when he saw me. "Hey-a, Boomi-girl."

"Hey, Denny."

"You okay there?" he asked.

"Yeah." I looked more closely at his coat—long, gray, and made of wool. All at once, it clicked—I knew where I'd seen it before. "Is that my dad's coat?"

"Sure is. He made a box of things for me last winter. Trudging through hell at that hospital, but still took the time to think of me. That's the kinda dude your dad was. . . . Hey, you know you're not supposed to be out here after dark."

Once, Denny disappeared for three weeks and came back with a haircut. Some days, Denny didn't want to talk, or talked to people no one could see. Those were bad days. Today, I could tell, was a good day.

I stared at the door to our building. I knew I had to go up, but I liked it out there, in the crisp, open air.

He ran his fingers through his scraggly beard. "You miss him, huh?"

I shrugged. "Yeah."

"Well, when I talked to him the other day—"

"What?" A shiver ran up my arms. "What do you mean you talked to him?" Was this one of his bad days, when he heard people who weren't there? "When did you talk to him? How?"

"Aw, Boomi-kid. Coulda been yesterday, coulda been last year. Time is just a story we tell ourselves. Makes us feel like we control the spin, when really we're just starfish in a whirlpool, hanging on for the ride."

"Oh." Tears sprang to my eyes, which was stupid. What was I expecting?

"Listen up, Boomi-girl. You listening?" I nodded. "He gave me this . . ." He dug into his sack, like an off-season Santa Claus. ". . . to give to you." He hauled out a cruddy old box. But it wasn't a box—it was a radio. An old yellow radio with an antenna sticking up, and a little see-through door.

"It's a boombox," Denny said. "Tape's inside, all ready to go."

"A tape? What's a tape?"

Denny pressed a button that opened the little door on the boombox, revealing a rectangular object.

"This, my friend, is a tape. Or a cassette. Or a cassette tape. Anyway, it plays music." Denny took it out and handed it to me. It sat lightly in my hands. It smelled like chemicals and dust. Spanning its front was an old sticky label that read *Radio Mix One*. Something about that phrase echoed in my chest. I'd heard it before, but I couldn't remember where. "Looky here," Denny said. He showed me the button on the boombox with the sideways triangle. If I pushed it, the tape would play.

"My dad gave this to you?" I asked. It felt like a miracle— something new from Dad, when I'd thought there was nothing left.

"To give to *you*, Brown Eyes."

"But why give it to you? Why not my mom? Or me?"

"I think you'd know better than I would. But hold on! He wanted me to tell you something."

"What?"

Denny went quiet, then blinked at me. "What?"

"What else did he want to tell me, Denny?"

"Oh, right, yeah. Uh . . . let's see. Nope. Forgot."

"Denny!"

"Sorry, kid. I got a mind like a cheese grater."

He tugged at a lock of hair, like he was trying to yank his memory loose. "Hold on!" he shouted. "Here it comes! Wait for iiiiiit . . . wait for iiiit . . . batteries!"

"Batteries?"

"Definitely, probably, something about batteries."

"Oh. Right." So the thing needed batteries. This was Dad's big message? I grabbed the boombox. "Thanks anyway." I walked up my steps, my bones heavier than ever. "Good night, Denny."

"You get on home, Boomi-girl." He crossed his arms, closed his eyes, and started singing to himself.

I let myself into our house and up our narrow, dark staircase.

In the kitchen, Mom was rinsing greens under the tap. A tower of dirty dishes sat next to her. "Good day or bad day?" she asked. She'd seen me talking to Denny. Sometimes, she sent food down for him.

"Good day, I think. Maybe not. I couldn't tell." Denny didn't eat on his bad days, but she'd probably take him a plate, anyway. After my own bad day, I could have eaten twelve cheeseburgers.

Once, a few years ago, when the wind rattled our door and temperatures dropped below freezing, Dad went out into the night and brought Denny back with him. Denny had slept in Mom's office and left the next morning. I'd asked Mom why he couldn't just move in with us, and Mom said we couldn't solve all the world's problems. But that night, I heard her talking to Dad, and a few weeks later, Denny told me he had a brand-new sleep-home, a shelter with a hot breakfast and a bed for him. He's been going there ever since.

Mom turned around and saw the boombox. "Oh, lord. I told you not to take stuff from him, Boomi."

"It was a gift." I didn't say from who. From *whom*. I don't think she knew it used to be Dad's. I wrapped it in my coat, suddenly protective.

"We don't need other people's junk." She turned back to the sink. And *that*, my friend, is exactly why Dad didn't give the boombox to Mom. She's the queen of throwing stuff away. It's her favorite hobby. "Say hi to Paati," she ordered, "and go take a shower."

"It needs batteries," I told her.

"Good luck with that."

TRACK 4
My Life

What else can I tell you about myself? My name means earth in Sanskrit, which is an ancient Indian language. I have a faint mustache that I can't wait to get rid of and a dimple on my left cheek. My eyes are brown. I like my eyes. I can do nine cartwheels in a row before I get dizzy and have to stop. I get along with most people, and I usually have friends. I'm not the best student, but I'm not the worst.

My favorite subject is grammar. Is that weird? Commas and quotations, semicolons and apostrophes, uppercase and lowercase, underlines and italics. I like having rules and sticking to them. I like knowing how things should be and then knowing that that's how they *will* be. Maybe that's why I like ballet so much. There's an exact, precise way to place my feet, to hold my arms. Things are correct or incorrect, and everyone knows the rules.

What happened to Paati, though, seems very much against the rules. Paati is my dad's mom, and when I was little, the doctors told her she had something called dementia, which means that parts of her memory had broken down. She could talk, but she almost never did. Sometimes, I caught a glimmer in her eye, like she was about to say something. But then she didn't. I wished she would. On the plus side, she never said anything when I changed the channel.

In the living room, Rosario, the day nurse, was putting on her coat. "Good night, Mrs. Gopalan! Night, Boomi!" she called. Paati sat in her armchair in front of the television, brushing her hair. It cascaded down her shoulder, as white as whipped cream. She carried a big round paddle brush wherever she went, and brushing her hair was her favorite thing to do.

I went over to Paati's chair, and I made sure not to look at the fireplace mantel, at the ornate green box sitting there. I crouched next to her and took her hand. Her fingers hung limply in mine, and she stared straight ahead at a documentary about sharks. "Hey, Paati," I said, trying to sound cheerful. "I bombed my audition. I literally *fell* onstage." Her eyebrows jumped. "So, I didn't make the Studio Company and Mom's pissed." I took a deep breath and stared at a shadow in the corner. *Go on*, the shadow said, *tell us all about it.* "That means I can't do ballet anymore. But I'm trying not to think about that. I'm really super annoyed with that. And with stupid Madame Fontaine. And with myself. And with pointe shoes."

I stood up. And when I did, my eyes fell on that green box. I looked away. That box held Dad's ashes and I hated it.

If my life were grammar, that box would be totally, completely against the rules. But life isn't grammar, so the box just sat there, day after day, watching us leave for work and school, watching *Family Feud* with Paati. Now Paati was watching me. Something flickered behind her eyes. Her gaze fell on the yellow boombox. She lifted a finger and pointed at it.

"Just some junk from Denny," I said. She raised an eyebrow, like she didn't believe me, then went back to watching her show.

When Mom called me to dinner, I sat in my usual seat, across from Dad's usual seat, which, of course, was empty. Next to Dad's seat was Paati's. She ate way before us, but Mom insisted on walking her over from her armchair every evening, so we could eat dinner as a family.

Dinner that night was baked chicken. It sat on my plate, as bare as a bad apology. Next to it sat a sad clump of spinach. Paati gazed at my plate. She didn't look impressed.

I sniffed it. It smelled like the compost bin. "I'm not trying to do no Weight Watchers, Mom."

"Boomi."

"What's with the diet food, though?"

"It's a healthy meal made with love."

I speared the entire chunk of chicken and held it up to her. "Diet. Food."

"Well. You're on a diet."

"I am?"

Mom didn't answer. She just chewed her chicken and stared at the wall. When I followed her eyes, though, I found that she wasn't just staring at the wall, but at the pictures on the wall, and at one picture in particular. In it, Mom and Dad stood on a snowy sidewalk, Dad's arms wrapped sideways around her, Mom's mouth open with laughter. They both wore leather jackets, and Mom's hair blew around her head, like it was caught in a gale of wind. The picture was a little blurry, but their smiles were clear enough. Mom seemed to get lost in the picture, like she was back there again, living in that day.

On the wall, below the picture of Mom and Dad, was one of Dad when he was a little kid, sitting in a photo studio, next to a girl in braids. Archana. Archie Aunty. Dad's sister. She's a few years older than Dad, with big eyes, her mouth set in a straight line. She has a dimple on her left cheek, same as mine. I've never met her. She sends us a holiday card every year—not a photo card, but the boring kind with a picture of a snowman or a tree. Every year, she scrawls the same message. *Happy Christmas! Yours—A.* I used to ask Dad about her—where was she? Did she live in England still? Did she have kids? How come we never saw her? Did she not like us?

When Dad died, we had an online memorial. I read a poem. People logged on, pages and pages of little rectangles, each containing the head of someone who loved Dad. I clicked through the pages of people, searching for one in particular. On the third page, I saw her name: Archana Gopalan. But she was a black box. She was watching but hadn't turned her own camera on. When the memorial ended, she logged off right away, and was gone.

A few days after the memorial, a bouquet of flowers arrived at our door—white lilies, a little brown around the edges. I barely looked at them at first, but it was the way Mom picked them up, the way she stared quietly at the little gift card, that caught my eye. I snatched the card from her before she could stop me. *Regrets for not being more involved*, it read. *Was traveling for work. Sending deepest sympathies and best wishes, Archie.* Archie! I should have been glad she sent these, glad to see her name. But something didn't feel right.

"No personal pronouns," I said to Mom.

"What?"

"She never uses the word *I*. Like *I'm sorry*. Or *I miss you*. Or *I love*—"

"Yes, okay. I see what you're saying. It is a bit . . ." Mom trailed off. She didn't have to finish her sentence.

We ate our dinner and the house fell silent, except for the click-clack of Paati's dentures, the tap and scratch of Mom's fork against her plate, the occasional groan of an engine on the street. I could feel them, the shadows, inching toward the table, slinking over Dad's empty chair. The people next door, the ones who owned the yellow half of the house, were having some kind of dinner party. Through the kitchen wall, I could hear voices and the beep of a microwave. I heard a chair scrape against the floor, a brief silence, and then an explosion of laughter. They had dinner parties a lot. They also had matching red Vespas. Mom said you could have those sorts of things when you didn't have kids. I'd rather they had kids.

Mom slammed her fork down then, like she'd had enough. I waited for her to say something, but she didn't. She just took a deep breath. Then she retied the yellow scarf around her head. One curl sprang from the cloth and flopped over her eyes. Across from me, Paati contemplated the table silently. I chewed on my baked chicken and fought to swallow it. It was like eating a sock.

Have you ever tried chewing on food that just won't get any smaller? Sitting at the table, staring past Mom at Archie's picture, I chewed that chunk of chicken until my jaw hurt. The meat just got tougher, like it was mad at me, like it was trying to turn back into a chicken. I thought of spitting it out, but I'd get in trouble for that. So I hoped for the best and swallowed. The hard little fist of flesh inched down my throat—and then it stopped. Stuck. I tried to swallow again to force it down, but it wouldn't budge. It just sat there, dry and mean. I gagged. Paati noticed first. She slapped her palm against the table.

"Boomi!" Mom jumped from her chair and whacked me on the back, which hurt and didn't help. I grabbed for my glass of milk and gulped it down, but all that did was make me cough so hard that the chunk of chicken and a splatter of milk flew right across the table and hit Dad's empty chair. Paati stared at the chewed-up glob of food, then stared back at me.

I burst out crying. Mom grabbed a napkin, crouched on

the floor, and started to wipe my face. "No!" I shoved her hand away. "Stop that!"

She lowered her hand and stared at me. "What's wrong?" Her eyes were wide and scared. I sat there, gagging and sniffling. "This is stupid."

"What is?"

"This dumb dinner. And nobody talking. And this chicken. It's all terrible and horrible and I'm tired of it!" My words rang through the kitchen. Mom sat back down. The shadows gathered around, waiting to see what happened next. For a long time, nothing happened. Mom just stared at her lap.

Then, finally, she screeched her chair back and stood. Paati looked up in alarm. *Yell at me*, I thought silently. *Yell so I can yell back. At least then there'd be noise.* But Mom didn't yell. Instead, she raised her fist to her forehead, closed her eyes, and took a deep breath. Finally, she opened them again.

"Thank you for your thoughts," she said. She sat back down and picked up her knife and fork. "Finish your spinach, at least." With that, she cut into her meat, lumped it with spinach, and went on eating. Next door, the sounds of the dinner party carried on, the clinking and laughter, like nothing at all had happened.

TRACK 5
The Number One Song in Heaven

After dinner, my throat still raw from choking, I logged onto Mom's computer and typed into the search bar: *When someone dies.* The search engine tried to finish my question for me:

What happens to their soul?

Where do they go?

Without a will

What to say

On your birthday

None of the questions were my question, so I filled in the rest myself: *how long does it take to feel better?* The shadows slinked over from their corners and gathered around me, waiting for the answer. The first answer: *There is no fixed timeline for grief . . . anywhere from six months to four years.*

Four years? Four years seemed like an extremely long time. And what made them so sure about four years? Was I going to wake up when I was fifteen and not feel so bad? Would I start the tenth grade and stop missing him? I wasn't sure I wanted that. I wasn't sure at all.

When the pandemic started, the world shut down and moved online. Dad, though—he just kept going to work, along with other doctors and nurses. Day after day at that hospital, week after week. It's like the rest of us were running away from a fire, and they were running straight in. But I tried not to think about that. I tried not to think about my dad running into the fire.

One day, he came home from the hospital with a fever. He knew right away what it was. We shut him in Mom's office and left meals for him outside the door.

At first, we weren't that worried. Dad was healthy and sort of young. We thought for sure he'd get a little sick and then get better. My mom got it, and she got better. I even got it, and I barely had a sniffle. And for a while, Dad seemed to be getting better, too. I remember sitting on a bench with him outside Boba Dreams, which, like lots of places, was open for pick-up orders. I'd just had Covid, so I didn't have to isolate from him. Dad stuck his straw up his mask when he sipped. I remember sitting on a bench with him outside Boba Dreams. I'd gotten a milk tea with exploding mango boba, and he had a green tea with lychee boba. We played Would You Rather. "Would you rather have free boba for the rest of your life or never have to do homework again?" he asked.

"Free boba. Would you rather talk out of your butt or eat with your toes?"

"Oh, definitely talk out of my butt. No question. I do that

anyway." That made me laugh.

I shut Mom's laptop now. The shadows had lost interest and gone back to their corners. In case you're wondering, the shadows were exactly that. Shadows. They moved in when Dad died, and they didn't show any signs of leaving. They were human-shaped, but they didn't have faces. Just round heads and wispy arms and legs. They stalked around the house and asked dumb questions. They were basically useless, but aside from Paati and Mom and Archie Aunty, they were my closest relatives.

Back in my room, I stood in front of the mirror and took a good long look at myself, at the body that, according to Madame Fontaine, was not made for ballet. We'd done okay so far, me and this body. When I danced, it didn't feel too big.

I raised one arm to my side, at a perfect 85-degree angle. I did a rond de jambe, moving my pointed foot in a slow semi-circle. Maybe it hadn't been such a bad day—I got to dance for six whole hours, after all.

I thought of the bodies I saw at the Academie Fontaine— the framed dancers on the walls, so thin I could see every bone and tendon in their necks; Bebe Jacobs with her long legs, her twiggy arms. I rolled up my sleeves. My own arms bulged out at the top. My neck was thick and my waist was wide. I had an extra pocket of fat on my knees.

If Dad were here, he'd kiss the top of my head. *They can keep their twiggy arms*, he'd say. If Dad were here, he'd tell me not to worry about what I looked like, not to worry about the

Academie Fontaine. He'd pull me away from this mirror and take me on a walk around the neighborhood. We'd go to Boba Dreams.

I imagined myself growing and growing, getting wider and taller and filling up my room, cracking through the ceiling. If I kept growing, would I fill the emptiness that Dad had left behind? Would the shadows stop asking for him? Could I get big enough to make up for a whole other person, a whole Dad?

I closed my eyes, thought of him, and let my arms rise again. My heel met my toe. I could feel the pull of the tendons in my feet, and I knew they were in a perfect fifth position. I could hear the tumble of piano keys in my head. I moved through my alignments, then moved into that day's audition piece, a petit allegro, from glissade to jeté to pas de chat to soubresaut. I could name the steps, but when I danced, those names fell away, and the dance became its own perfect storm, a quiet tornado with no beginning or end. When I danced, *I* had no beginning or end.

Then my eyes opened, and I got the feeling I'd sometimes get—like my insides were a dark and windy cave. Nothing—not screen time, or dance, or even a trip to Boba Dreams—could make me feel better. That's how I felt that night. I thought maybe I should pray, but I didn't know who to pray to. We weren't religious. We didn't go to temple.

One day, when Dad was sick and isolated in the office, I sat just outside the tiny crack in the door. I was starting to worry about him. He was getting worse. He woke up from a nap, and he must have sensed me sitting there. "Booms?"

"Dad," I said. "How come we don't go to temple? We're Hindu, right?"

"Technically," he said.

"Do you not believe in God?"

"I wouldn't say that."

"Does God exist?"

"He'd have to be pretty impressive, if He did."

"Who says He's a *he*?" I asked.

"You're right. Who said He's even a single being? It's possible God is something the human brain can't comprehend."

"Like if we saw Him, our brains would explode."

"Immediately."

We sat and thought about this for a while. "That's not very reassuring, is it?" he asked. "Let's give God a name. Something our brains can comprehend. What's the greatest thing? The most powerful, impressive thing in the world?"

"Boba," I said.

"No. Boba is not the most impressive thing."

"The sun."

"The earth?"

"The ocean."

"The atmosphere."

"I don't like any of those," I said. "I can't comprehend *the atmosphere*. That's just as confusing as *God*."

"What are your favorite things?"

"Dance and Bebe and you and Mom and Paati. And boba. And grammar tests. What are *your* favorite things?"

"Burritos. And you."

"Burritos are all wrapped up and plain looking, but on the inside they contain, like, everything. Like the universe."

"Burritos it is, then," Dad said. He raised a hand and closed his eyes. "I hereby declare the founding of the Church of the Big Burrito. May He rule this Earth with peace and—and—"

"Good salsa," I cut in.

"And good salsa."

"Not the red chunky kind."

"Not the red chunky kind. Maybe a nice tomatillo." He stopped to think. "Who says the Big Burrito is a *he*, though?"

"He just is. Burri-*to*. It would be Burri-*ta* if He was a lady."

"Who says the Big Burrito has any gender at all?" Dad asked.

Now, I kneeled down at my bed and folded my hands, like children in storybooks. I tried to think of the Big Burrito. Safe and warm, full of good things. Then I stopped thinking of the Big Burrito and just thought of Dad.

A loud knock on the door and Mom flung it open. Why knock if she was just going to open it anyway?

"Just so you know," she said, "I did a kitchen clean-out and I've thrown out all our sweets."

I stared at her. "All of them?"

"Yes."

"The ice cream?"

"Yes."

"The Girl Scout cookies in the freezer?"

"Yup."

"What about my Halloween candy?"

"Gone."

"WHY?"

"You're changing, Boomi. It's just a fact of life. Your body's changing and you don't get to eat like you did when you were little. Did you see the girls in your audition group? Bebe Jacobs? Do you think she eats whatever she feels like? Chocolate and ice cream? No!"

"I know for a fact that Bebe Jacobs eats whatever she feels like. Today at lunch she had a french-fry-and-ketchup sandwich."

Mom raised her fist to her forehead and breathed out hard. This is what she does when she's about to lose it but is trying not to. I didn't get what she was so mad about. *She* threw away *my* Halloween candy. *I* should have been angry. "I don't want you to miss any more opportunities because of your weight, Boomi. Ballerinas take care of their bodies. They eat what they need to eat to be dancers."

"Well, maybe I'm not a dancer."

"Don't say that." She sighed. "Please. Just try. Okay?"

"Try what?"

She crossed her arms, stared at me for a few seconds, and left.

TRACK 6
Cruel Summer

Late that night, I zinged awake, my stomach gurgling. My mouth tasted chalky and sour and begged for something sweet. My clock read midnight. I thought back to dinner, to the lousy chicken that almost killed me. Through the midnight gloom, I could see a long, dry year of Mom food. Chicken breasts. Wilted spinach. Nonfat yogurt. *You don't get to eat like you did when you were little.*

"That's what she thinks," I whispered. She *thought* she'd cleaned out all the sweets, but she didn't know about the piano bench. Last Halloween, we bought candy, because people were trick-or-treating, even during quarantine. But hardly anyone rang our bell. We had a whole bag of chocolate mini-bars left over. I'd rescued them before Mom could hide them away, and stuck them in the piano bench. I'd planned to share them with Bebe.

Creeping across the quiet house, into the living room, I lifted the lid of the bench and there they were. I chose my favorite kind, plain milk chocolate, and unwrapped it. I was just going to have one, so it had to be the best one.

Bebe Jacobs and I had been dancing together since we were Tutu Tots at the Academie Fontaine. The first day of our first class, I stood next to her at the barre. She turned and looked me right in the eye. I said, "You want to be friends?" She nodded, and the rest was history. Until yesterday.

I dug out a Nestlé Crunch and ate that, too. Then a Krackel.

When the Academie Fontaine shut its doors, Bebe and I started meeting on Zoom to work on our dance challenges. We were learning all the TikTok dances we could, and we were getting pretty good. We learned "Chicken Noodle Soup," then "Say So," "Git Up," and "Renegade," but "Chicken Noodle Soup" was always my favorite.

And then, the day after Dad died, I missed our usual meeting time, and when I went back the next day, Bebe wasn't there. I practiced the dances on my own, but it wasn't the same. Sometimes I'd try to chat with her online, but she never answered. Mom said that Bebe didn't have her own phone, so she was probably just missing my messages.

Last fall, when ballet started again, our class split into pods and moved into a corner of Golden Gate Park. Bebe wasn't in my pod, and even if she were, we would have had to stay six feet apart from each other. Hard to be two peas in a pod when you're standing six feet apart.

I found a Mr. Goodbar. These were the friendliest of all

the bars, with their yellow-and-red wrappers, the peanuts that were just happy to be there.

Yesterday, when I walked into the audition room, I spotted Bebe right away. "Beebs! You got new shoes!" Her ballet slippers were black. She'd been wanting them for months, but her mom was making her grow out of her old pink ones first. "Your feet grew!"

I ran right up to her, ready to hug her, then halted. She looked at me like she barely knew me. It was like she'd put up a wall that I slammed into. Around her stood a group of girls I'd never talked to before. I'd seen them at Fontaine, too, but they'd been in different classes, and they were a little older. From their perfectly wound buns to their sleek black slippers, they were as long and slim as greyhounds. Just like Bebe. I looked down at my own baby-pink shoes, my white tights with dark smudges at the knees. I remembered Mom sighing and tutting over my leotard that morning, pulling at the shoulders. I was suddenly very aware of my belly, the way it bulged over my legs.

Bebe stared at my smudged knees. "I didn't know you were auditioning with us."

"Yeah, you did. We talked about it all last year."

She gave the other girls an embarrassed sort of grin. "Um . . . I meant I didn't know you'd be in this group." She laughed a little—at what?—and walked off. Weirdly, the other girls followed. How did that happen?

I ate another plain milk chocolate, another Krackel, a Mr. Goodbar, and a Special Dark. This time, I let them melt against the roof of my mouth before breaking them with my tongue. I ate three more after that and then three more. The more I ate, the more I wanted, and the better I felt.

A few times during auditions, I caught Bebe staring at me. The first time, I smiled at her. She looked quickly away. During our lunch breaks, Bebe sat in a tight huddle with the other three girls. Can you sometimes tell when people are talking about you? Bebe said something and one of her new friends turned around to look at me, then whipped back to face the group. They stooped over in hushed giggles. I ate lunch both days with another group of girls. I didn't know their names, but it was easy enough to just shut up and clump into their group. Better than eating alone. It wasn't like me, by the way, to shut up and clump in. Bebe had turned into someone I didn't recognize. But weirdly, so had I.

I ate another and another. Everything about that chocolate felt good—the wrapper smooth against my fingers, the tiny tear of paper when I opened it, the shine of its aluminum inner shell, the perfect rectangle of perfect chocolate, each piece a little different from the last. But not too different. Eating that candy was like eating a hug, and so I ate and ate and ate.

When I reached back into the big bag, the chocolates were gone. *Impossible,* I thought. But when I held the bag up, it was just a skin of empty plastic. Around me spread a sea of crumpled wrappers. I stuffed them back in the bag, stuffed the bag deep in the kitchen garbage can, and went back to bed, no closer to sleep than I'd been before.

TRACK 7
Jump!

Back in bed, I dipped into a shallow, buzzy slumber, and then a dream. In my dream, I was reading a stack of letters from Dad. Dozens of them. Piles and piles of them. But the strange thing was, I couldn't read any of the words. Each time I locked eyes on a sentence, it swam away from me. It happened over and over until finally, one word jumped to the surface: *boombox*. I sat straight up in bed. There was something about that boombox. Why else would Dad save it for me?

I pulled it down from my shelf. Its yellow was covered in a layer of dark, sticky grime. I peered into the little door, opened and closed it. "Okay," I said. "Let's see what you can do."

I pressed play.

Nothing happened. I pressed stop.

I pressed play again.

Nothing.

I sighed and kicked the boombox onto its side. Of course

nothing happened. Nothing ever happens. The idea of something new, something special from Dad, had frothed up like a glorious bubble bath. But one by one, the bubbles started popping. Why would Dad give me a dingy old radio? And what did I expect a dingy old radio to do? And why give it to Denny, not straight to me or Mom? Each question I asked popped another bubble. This radio wasn't a gift from Dad. It was an old piece of junk, a souvenir of Denny's bad day.

Then I remembered: batteries. I flipped the radio over and found the battery compartment. It was going to be empty, of course. Or if it had batteries in it, they'd be crusty old things from the eighties. Would batteries from the eighties still work? I struggled with the battery compartment, trying to lever the lid off with my fingernail. Finally—*pop!*—the lid flew open. Inside, no batteries. But it wasn't empty. Something else was in there: a piece of paper, folded up and wedged in the hole. My heart thudded. I pulled the note out, unfolded it. My heart thudded. Carefully, I pulled the stiff folds apart until the note lay flat. There, at its center, a single sentence: *You can change your life.*

I recognized Dad's handwriting, his big fat *Y* and the flat, short *o*'s *and u*'s. He had put this here for me before he gave it to Denny. But why? What could I do with it? How had he known I'd find it? I closed the battery compartment and flipped the boombox back over. There was only one thing left to do. I took a breath, closed my eyes, and said the sentence

out loud, like it was a magic spell. "You can change your life."
I pressed the play button again. I waited.

I sat for a minute in my dark and silent room. A car passed
on the street. The wind howled.

And then I heard a click. The tiniest, quietest click.

It came from the boombox. The click was followed by
a low *shhhhhhhh*. I peered through the little window at the
cassette. The two round wheels were rolling—the tape was
playing. *Shhhhhh*. And then, out of the hush: the shout of a
drum, a keyboard hopping up and down a scale, and a woman's voice that punched into the quiet night.

"It's working," I whispered. It was *loud*. Mom would hear!
I lunged for the boombox, but before I reached it, it jumped!
It hopped right off the floor, like a juiced-up toaster. I backed
away and it hopped at me again. The voice filled the room
now. "Quiet!" I hissed. But the voice only grew. The boombox
started to shake, to bop to the music, and as it did, a puddle of
light formed under it, then started to spread. It seeped closer
and closer, until it lapped at my toes. I climbed up and stood
on my bed, watching the light get brighter and spill across the
floor, then crawl up the walls. Soon, I couldn't see the walls
or the floor or even my own hand. The light swallowed everything. I needed Mom. I needed her to stop this.

"Mom!" I called. Now I was hoping she'd hear, hoping
she'd open my door and rescue me from whatever this was. I
could still escape, shut the door to this room and run to Mom's.
I jumped from my mattress—and froze, midair. Around me,

the room seemed to drain of color. I saw a FLASH. I heard a BOOM. Then, nothing but deep, dreamy silence. The room grew as still as a photograph, suspended in a golden pool of light.

Look, I wouldn't believe me, either. I'm just telling you what happened, and you can believe me or not. After the boom, I floated for a while, and then I stopped floating and started falling. As I fell, a sort of tunnel formed around me and I started to see things—little movies, swirling all around me. Here's what I saw:

A boy at his desk, hunched over a textbook.

A teenage girl bolting up from that table, her chair banging to the ground.

A woman sitting alone at the table, eating rice with her hand. Before her sat several bowls of steaming, barely touched food and two empty plates. Beside her sat two empty chairs.

I kept falling, down and down, until, at last, I crashed to the ground. My head spun and my stomach lurched. When my eyes opened, all I could see was a haze of white and red, a few big blurry objects in the room. My palms scraped against rough carpet. In the distance, very faintly, I heard the same song that had been playing on the boombox. Slowly, my eyes started to focus. I sat up. Below me: red carpet. Beside me: a gold-and-white armchair. I fingered the row of gold tassels that dangled from its lower edge, then ran my hand over its velvet covering. I had no idea where I was. Across the room sat a television—I think it was a television. It was the sort of television I'd seen in old picture books—a squat brown box with a gray screen, dials on its edge, antennae sticking off the top of it. This was someone's house—someone's silent, empty, cold house. I lumbered to my feet and almost fell again but caught hold of a wall for balance. It was solid. It was real. It was covered in a fuzzy red-and-white wallpaper. I'd never *ever* been in a house with fuzzy wallpaper.

"Hello," I whispered. No one heard me. I tried again, louder. "Hello?" On top of the television sat a tiny replica of the Taj Mahal, and beside it, a portrait of two children. Two children I recognized.

My heart leaped and spun in its cage. A girl and a boy, side by side, in a gold frame. I knew that picture. I knew that boy.

"Ooohhhh . . ." A frightened moan seeped out of my mouth. This was not right. This was not okay. "Okay," I said aloud. Why was I talking out loud? "Okay . . . um . . . this is fine. This is okay. This is probably just a dream." I walked from the living room into a kitchen, where a yellow fridge hummed. A box lay toppled over on the countertop. A trail of milk led to a bowl of half-eaten soggy cereal. I walked over and set the box upright. *Ricicles*, it read. I felt like Goldilocks. Whose cereal was this? Baby bear's, I hoped.

BRRRRIIIIIIIING! I jumped. Next to the fridge, a boxy thing on the wall was ringing. A phone. This was a phone. It was the loudest thing I'd ever heard.

Footsteps thumped down the hallway and then, all at once,

in the flesh: a boy. He wore enormous glasses. He had floppy, curly black hair. He was exactly my height. In his hand, he held a pencil, which he raised now, like a dagger. "Dad?"

Fear flashed in his eyes. "Mum!" he yelled. "Mum! Mummy!!" Then he stopped yelling and stood there, staring at me. In his eyes, fear turned to confusion. He lowered the pencil. I could hardly breathe, looking at him. I never thought I'd see Dad again. But here he was, right in front of me, the same height as me, the same age. It was so completely *him.*

His eyes swept over the room. "How'd you get in here?"

All I could do was shake my head.

"How'd you get in my house?"

I gulped. "I don't know."

"Did you break in? Listen to me. If you broke a window—"

"I didn't—" I couldn't tell him the truth, that I'd fallen, somehow, from the ceiling.

"Why are you glowing?" he asked.

"What?"

"You're glowing."

I looked down and he was right. My clothes shimmered with a thin film of light. The little hairs on my arms sparked from their tips. I stared at the boy. He stared at me. For a long time, he was quiet. And then:

"Hold it. Are you an alien?" He dropped the pencil and raised his hands like he was about to do karate on me. "Don't hurt me," he said breathlessly. "Please. I'll take you to our leader."

"I'm from California," I said, like that explained anything.

He stared at me a second longer. "Hollywood?"

"No. San Francisco."

He lowered his hands. "You're not going to axe-murder me, are you? Or do alien experiments on my brain?"

"No."

That settled it for him. His shoulders sank. He folded his arms. "You seem all right," he said. "I mean, you're clearly dodgy in some way, but you're not going to suck my brains out."

"Definitely not."

When I looked down again, the glow had faded away.

He walked over to the counter, picked up the box of Ricicles, and took his bowl to the sink. Then he turned back to me.

"And you came here, from *America*. You left *California* to come to England. On purpose. Did I get that right?"

"Yeah."

"On holiday."

"Sure." I started to relax a little, too.

"What's your name?" he asked.

"Boomi."

"Boomi. That's an odd name."

"It means earth."

He thought about this for a few seconds. "Well, come along, Boomi from California." He turned and started back down the hallway. I followed him. We passed one bedroom, then another, then a big sort of closet with clothes drying in it, but no one else was around.

"Aren't your parents home?" I asked.

"Guess not."

"Where's your mom?"

"Out."

"Out where?"

"Gosh, I don't know, the shops, probably."

"Where's your dad?"

"Not here."

"Oh—" Something tickled my memory. "You mean—"

"He's dead. Brown bread. Popped his clogs. Snuffed it."

"Got it. Glad you're able to talk about it."

The boy—Dad—shrugged. "It's been a long time. I don't really remember him." Dad's dad died of a heart attack when Dad was very young. I'd known that. I just sort of . . . forgot.

We reached the end of the dark corridor and Dad banged through a door and into a bedroom—his bedroom. It was the bedroom I'd seen as I fell through the time tunnel, complete with a small desk in the corner, covered in books.

"You're studying," I said. "I thought it was summer break."

He stared at his desk, like he was just noticing it. Then he turned to me. "Where are you staying? In Thumpton?"

"What's your name?" I asked, batting away his question. I knew his name, obviously. It was Jeevan.

"Jimmy." *Jimmy!*

"No, it's not!"

41

"It's what I call myself."

"Since when?"

"Since keep-your-nose-out-of-it, Boomi. If that's even *your* real name." I knew, for sure, that I wouldn't be calling him Jimmy. He flopped down on the carpet and pulled on something hidden under his bed. "You've interrupted me."

"Doing what?"

From under his bed he pulled a boombox. "Hid this here when I thought you were a robber," he said. *My boombox.* Only here, now, it was bright yellow, shiny and new. He must have seen the look on my face. "What's wrong?" he asked.

"Where'd you get that?"

"Birthday present." He patted it proudly. "She's one week old today."

Normal, Boomi. Act normal. "So—you said—what were you doing?"

"I was making a mix tape. Do you know what that is? Do they have them where you're from?"

I shook my head.

"Really?"

"I guess I've heard the word, but I don't know what it is."

For a few seconds, he stared at me like I really was an alien. And then he started talking again. I watched more than I listened. As he talked, he seemed to forget that I'd *literally* dropped into his life from nowhere. He turned on his radio. A soap commercial led into a cereal commercial and then a DJ's crisp voice introduced a song. I'd heard it somewhere before. "Oh, I know this one!"

"Shhhh!" He hushed me with one finger. "I've got to get the exact . . ." He pressed two buttons down. "There. Got it. It's recording now." From there, Jeevan started talking about radio mixes versus mix tapes. What he was making, technically, was a radio mix, because it was just a tape full of songs that he'd recorded off the radio. Radio mixes, you made for yourself. They had the ragged ends of commercials and DJ's voices hanging off them. You just waited for a song you wanted, pressed record, and that was that. You could never choose the order you wanted; you were just lucky to catch the song you'd been waiting for. Mix tapes, though, were tapes you designed. You chose the order you wanted, the songs you wanted.

"You make them for your mates or if you meet someone who's really into the same music as you and you want them to hear stuff you like. Or you make one for the person you fancy," he said. "But I don't think I'll ever waste my time on that." And then he went on. And on. And on. I never thought one person could have so much to say about a plastic rectangle with two holes in it. I sat there pretending to listen, wondering why we got rid of tape players if they were so great, wondering if I should break the news to him about cell phones. Maybe if I told him, he could invent a cell phone and then one day, in the future, we'd be rich enough to buy the other side of our duplex and have our own dinner parties and matching Vespas.

I thought about riding around San Francisco on matching Vespas with Dad. And then I remembered the truth, and then I got very sad. Jeevan stopped talking.

"What's wrong now?"

"Nothing."

"Are you homesick for your planet?"

"Very funny."

"I know what'll cheer you up. I feel like a Wham Bar. You fancy a Wham Bar?" He jumped to his feet and went over to his dresser, where he picked up a piggy bank. But it wasn't the usual pink pig standing on all fours with a slot on its back. This one was a ceramic pig, its clay glazed and shiny, wearing a tuxedo, a red bow tie, and an open-mouthed smile. Jeevan pulled a black plug from its bottom and shook out an impressive pile of coins—silver and pale gold and copper. It looked like pirates' treasure. He scraped up a handful of coins and crammed them in his pocket. "Come along, then, Boomi from America." He yanked his bedroom window open and climbed through it. I don't know why he didn't just use the door, but I'd asked enough questions. I hoisted myself onto the sill and slid, feet first, onto the sidewalk below. He looked down at my socked feet. "Where are your shoes?"

My shoes were in 2021.

"No bother." He dove back through the window and emerged with a pair of rain boots. "Wellies will do. Rains every three seconds, anyway." Just as he handed me the boots, a storm of footsteps came thumping down the stairs.

44

"I'm going!" a voice called. It was a female voice. From someone young. But older than us.

Jeevan jumped to his feet and flung his door open. "Going where?" he shouted.

"Library!"

"No, you're not!"

"Keep out of it!"

"I refuse to lie for you!" he yelled. The only response was the slam of a door, footsteps fading down the sidewalk. Jeevan grumbled and closed his door. He glanced at me. "I won't be lying for her."

"For who? Who was that?" I asked.

"Keep your nose out of it. Get those wellies on."

"Rude."

He slipped out his window and down the road before I'd even stuck my feet into the boots. They were warm and heavy.

"Hang on!" I called, jogging to catch up with him. "Where'd you say we were going?"

He turned to me. "Sweetshop, just down the road." For the first time, he looked at me and smiled, a grin that stretched from one ear to the other, like a hammock. It was Dad's smile. Before I could stop myself, I reached over and hugged him.

"Oy! Get off!" he growled and pushed me away. "Is that what they do in San Francisco?"

"Sorry."

We walked on for a little while. The first thing I noticed was the air. The air here was wet and buzzed a little, like when you put your ear to something electric. I could smell rain. Jeevan's street was lined with a single nonstop brick wall, stamped every few feet with a front door. These were people's houses, crammed right up against each other. A sign stuck to the edge of the brick wall: Alphabet Street. I stopped. I knew this street. I knew it well.

TRACK 8
Life in a Northern Town

"Alphabet Street was like any other street in any other town in the middle of England," Dad said. He sat in the dark of my room, the edges of his face lit from the window, ghostly and pale in the moonlight. "But there was one very special thing about it. Every house on our street belonged to an Asian family."

"Like the Lees?"

"No—Asian like us. In Britain, *Asian* is what they call South Asians—Indians, Pakistanis, Sri Lankans, Bangladeshis, Nepalese, Bhutanese—"

"Dad."

"Yes? Oh, right." He cleared his throat. "In Thumpton, there was an old factory at the edge of town, made of brown bricks. Every morning at seven thirty-five, every front door on Alphabet Street would open, including ours. My mother would step out onto the sidewalk and join the river of people moving down our street, some old, some young, some chattering, some

47

quiet. Together they would walk all the way through town, until they reached the doors of the factory."

Dad's accent would get even more English when he talked about home. It would take on a sort of singsong bounce.

Mom used to read me actual bedtime stories, but Dad would just tell me about the things that had happened when he was a kid. Like the time he let his friend copy his test answers and they both got caught. Or the time he broke his neighbor's window with a soccer ball and had to scrub her bricks for six months to pay for its repair. Or the time the queen of England came sailing down his town's canals on some sort of royal tour, and the entire town gathered to wave to her.

"And I kid you not, Boomi, the queen of England looked right at me as her barge passed us by. She looked right at me and winked!"

"She did not! She probably had something in her eye."

I once asked Dad if Paati liked the factory, if she liked making those handkerchiefs and tablecloths. Dad smiled. "*Liking* was not the point, Boomi." People like Paati had to work where work was available. They would come home with sore hands and feet and heads, Dad said, but they'd always go back the next morning.

"Why didn't they just get a job they liked?"

"I suppose," he said, "they didn't care about *liking* their jobs. They did their jobs and that was it. *Liking* our jobs— that's what I got to do. That was Paati's gift to me."

I hadn't known, at the time, what Dad was talking about.

And I'm still not sure. But as Jeevan and I walked down Alphabet Street that first misty morning, I felt like I was stepping back into an old, familiar dream.

Alphabet Street was flat, missing the million little hills of my neighborhood. At the end of it rose an old brown church with a steeple that reached up and pierced the sky. In front of the church stood a giant oak tree, its branches fizzing with green, spreading wide and curving skyward.

As we passed the church, the street opened onto a square that was bordered by a row of shops, each with a painted sign in its window. The first one was Huston's Boiler's. For all your heating need's.

"Oh, no," I said, a thin spike of panic rising in me.

"What?"

"The apostrophes. They're all wrong."

"What are you talking about?"

"You don't need an apostrophe for plurals, just for possessives and contractions!"

Jeevan studied the sign. "It's just a sign. It gets the point across, don't it?"

"No, Jeevan!"

"Blimey, calm down, will you? And it's Jimmy."

"Jimmy, we're in England. Where English *started*. Who else is going to get the grammar right?"

Jeevan stared at me like I'd lost my mind. I had no idea, at that point, what waited for me. Store after store committed the same grammar crime. McAffrey's Appliance's.

Mary's Bap's and Biscuit's, for all your baked good need's. Branley's Fillet's and Loin's, for all your butchery need's. The shops went on and on. The whole block was an apostrophe catastrophe. That included the shop we stood in front of now: Winterbottom's News Agent's and Sweet's.

I shook my head. "For all your candy need's."

"Spot on!" Jeevan pushed the door open and a bell tinkled. An old man sat at the counter, flipping through a newspaper. "Hiya, Mr. Winterbottom."

Mr. Winterbottom half looked up, long enough to give me a suspicious stare and a grunt.

"He's an old grump," Jeevan muttered, leading me to the back of the shop. "But he's got the best sweets selection in Thumpton."

Jeevan wasn't lying. Before us rose a wall of sweets, bins filled with colorful hard candies, shelves stacked with bars and pouches of more candy, lollipops springing from buckets like daisies. He rattled off the names of the sweets. "You've got your Monkey Nuts, here. I don't fancy them much, but my sister does. Then your Yorkshire mix, your rhubarb-and-custards, sherbet lemons, Kola Kubes, refreshers, choco-limes, acid drops." Jeevan had grabbed a pink-and-white-striped bag and was shoveling sweets into it. He stopped, mid-scoop.

"Well, what's the matter now?"

"Nothing," I managed to say. I broke into a smile. A laugh welled up from my throat and flew into the room. Maybe it was being around all that candy. Maybe it was being here, with Dad. "Nothing's wrong!" I cried.

"You'd best keep quiet back there," came the croaky voice from the front.

"Sorry, Mr. Winterbottom." Jeevan grabbed a bar from the shelf. "Wham Bar," he said, and handed me one. "I'll have a Wham and a Marathon."

Back at the counter, Mr. Winterbottom put his paper down. I caught sight of the date: 14 July 1986. My arms started to tingle again. It was 1986. I looked around the shop, out the window, to see what 1986 looked like. I stuck my tongue out, the tiniest bit, to see what 1986 tasted like.

With a single shaky finger, Mr. Winterbottom punched some numbers into his cash register. A few white wisps of hair rose from his head like smoke. He puckered his lips into a sour sort of twist, like he'd just sucked on a lemon. Jeevan plunked some coins on the counter and the old shopkeeper slid back his change with the same bony, bent finger.

"Off with you, then," he said. But before he could shoo us away, he froze, listening. I listened through the quiet of the shop, and a moment later I felt a pulse, a distant drum, a deeply buried beating heart. I walked over to the glass door and put my ear to it.

"You there!" the shopkeeper hissed. "You'll be removing your grimy little ear from my door!"

"It's coming from outside," I said. I strained to hear and yes—there it was. Not a buried heart but a drumbeat, traveling through the air. It buzzed against my ear and faintly—*so* faintly—I could hear the up-down climb of melody, the sizzle of a drumbeat.

"Music," I said to Jeevan.

"You're right," Jeevan said, his eyes widening.

"Haven't got rid of him yet," Mr. Winterbottom grumbled. "The gall of that man!"

"What man?"

Jeevan and Mr. Winterbottom practically shouted the name in unison. "Disco Baba!" Jeevan was grinning. Winterbottom was not. Outside the sweetshop, the sound we'd heard began to take shape. *Boom-hiss-hiss-boom-hiss. Boom-hiss-hiss. Boom-hiss.*

Mr. Winterbottom peered out his window, blinking between the letters of his shop sign. "I'll be ringing the P&Q Commission, no doubt," he said. "He's the last of the problem, as I see it."

"What problem?" I asked.

Mr. Winterbottom ignored me. "Didn't half make a ruckus, did they?" he asked Jeevan. He turned to me. "You're not from here, so you wouldn't have seen it. They'd walk all over town, talking as loud as they liked. And dancing! Every holiday *dancing*! Out in the street! Carrying on like the devil's own! And don't get me started on the fireworks—"

Jeevan cut him off. "But they're not like that anymore. *We're* not, I mean." Jeevan seemed almost proud of this, like he'd been a good boy. Like he wanted a pat on the head.

"No," Mr. Winterbottom grunted, calming a little. "The commission put a stop to most of it. We're not that sort of town, you see. We're a quiet town."

"For quiet people," Jeevan said.

His eyes snapped to Jeevan. "Yes. That's right. For quiet people. The rest can take their infernal kerfuffle to London if they like."

"Their infernal kerfuffle?"

"Yes, that's right. Their infernal kerfuffle."

Outside, the *boom-hiss* was growing louder and closer, close enough now that we heard a melody. Jeevan turned to me and grinned. "We'd better catch him while we can."

Just then, a truck rolled into the town square. But this wasn't any old truck. This one was as pink as cotton candy. A giant soft-serve ice cream cone jutted cheerfully over its front window. Red and green tinsel fluttered from its bumper. Big silver baubles, like oversized Christmas ornaments, dangled from its roof. On its side, in swirly green letters, its sign read: Disco Baba's Ice Cream Wonders. The truck had pictures of cones and bars plastered to its side, just like any ice cream truck. But something was different about this one. Most ice cream trucks played the irritating songs I learned back in preschool. But this one was playing exactly what it promised: disco. A *boom-hiss* beat, a gale of a melody. No matter how you feel about disco, it made you want to shake your hips.

"Come on!" Jeevan grabbed my hand and pulled me out the door.

Mr. Winterbottom called after us, "He'll rue the day, he will!"

Jeevan ran at the truck, and I followed as well as I could in those clunky rain boots. By the time we got to it, a clutch of children had collected. They'd sprung from the pavement like dandelions, and now they danced and jumped around the truck's side window. And the wonders that passed through that window! Ice cream bars coated in rainbow sprinkles, cones crowned with vanilla soft serve, a wand of chocolate stuck into the sweet white cream. Sprinkle Top, Choc Top, Choc Flake, Flake Sherbet. The pictures on the side of the truck were unnaturally bright. Every few seconds, an arm emerged from the window, collected coins, and returned with an ice cream treat. Right on cue, my mouth started to water. I got that familiar feeling—a glow in my chest, a buzz in my hands—the feeling I'd had before eating a whole bag of chocolate minis. A single nervous thought of the bathroom scale tiptoed into my mind, but big loud shouts of ice cream chased it away.

We stood at the back of the line. In front of us gathered an impatient scrum of kids—where had they all come from? They were jostling and hopping up and down, tortured by the wait. But through it all, they barely made a sound. One by one, each kid stepped up to the window, peeped their order, took it, and scampered off. I was so busy watching, wondering at the total silence, that I didn't even notice it was our turn.

"Well?" I heard a high, throaty man's voice. "Chop, chop. I haven't got all day, you know." I looked up to find a brown man with jowls that hung from his cheeks like a bulldog's. A perfectly straight hedge of hair grew from his head. He wore giant sunglasses, gold rimmed, with rhinestones shining from the edges. His powder-blue pantsuit stretched over his sizable belly, and skinny arms stuck out from the short sleeves. He must have seen me staring at him, because he lowered his glasses and winked. "What will it be today, my duckies?"

Jeevan had to shout over the truck's engine. "A Choc Top with a Flake, please," he called. He squinted at me. "How about you? You want something?"

"Can I have—" I pointed to a picture.

"She'll have a sherbet top with raspberry sauce, please," Jeevan said.

The ice cream man nodded in my direction. "Who's this one, then?"

"Cousin," Jeevan answered.

This seemed like a good enough answer for Disco Baba. The ice cream man leaned farther out the window. "And your sister? Staying out of trouble?"

"Just about."

"You know it's three chances, my boy. She already has two penalties against her. Third time and she's out." Disco Baba disappeared into the truck. When he returned, he plunked a little wooden spoon into each soft head of ice cream. He had one last parting message for Jeevan: "She's a smart girl," he said. "Hopefully smart enough to keep her gob shut."

Jeevan just gazed up at the two cones in the ice cream man's hands, the ice cream of purest white, rising to a peak like a snowy mountain. "Ach," Disco Baba said. "No getting through to you now. Here you go. Off with you."

With a cone in my hand, the tangy, sweet raspberry sauce pricked my nose and made my mouth water. "He really is the best," Jeevan said. "I don't care that his music's ten years out of date. Or what Winterbottom thinks of him."

I took my first bite. It was like floating down a river of sweetness, a river of dreams and love and—I finally heard what Jeevan said. "What do you mean?" I asked. "What do people say?"

He shook his head. "Don't matter. This town is chockablock with old biddies who can't keep their noses out of other people's business."

We turned the corner, which led onto the big town square. From the far edge of the square, a stone bridge arched over a canal. We sat on a white bench. A sign for the Sunday market hung on a lamppost. That must have been the old market Dad had told me about. More signs dotted the square. Each was painted carefully onto a white wooden board, hung by hinges from a lamppost. WELCOME TO THUMPTON-ON-SOAR, one of them proclaimed. And below it, in smaller writing: A QUIET TOWN FOR QUIET PEOPLE. Another sign read, ABSOLUTELY, POSITIVELY NO LOITERING OR STREET PLAY. That would explain the quick disappearance of the children. And finally, a third sign warned, MIND YOUR P's AND Q's! At least they'd gotten the apostrophes right.

"What are P's and Q's?"

Jeevan dug a big wodge of ice cream from his cone and

stuck it in his mouth. He swallowed hard, winced at the cold. "It's the you-know-whos," he said, and went on mauling his ice cream cone.

"No. I don't know who. That's why I asked."

He wiped his mouth with his wrist. "The Peace and Quiet Commission," he said. "The people who don't like Disco Baba."

"I still don't get why people wouldn't like Disco Baba. I mean, I don't *love* disco, but the guy sells ice cream. How could you not love him?"

"It's not the ice cream, it's the noise." Jeevan slurped at the ice cream that dripped down his cone. He squinted at me, trying to figure me out. "You really want to know about the P's and Q's?"

"Yes."

"Okay," he began with a sigh. "All you really need to know is that they're a group of old toffs who try to boss the rest of us around. Like Mr. Winterbottom. He won't let more than two youths in his shop at once. Won't let you stand in front of the newsstand for more than five seconds, in case you're reading without buying. And says more-or-less racist things about Asians right to your face. But he's the one with the Wham Bars, so we keep going back. Next up, Theodora Gin-Bixby. Aka Ginger Biscuits. She'll offer you a biscuit whenever she sees you. Don't eat them. They're stale. Then there's Sybil Snodgrass. Snodgrass stalks the streets of Thumpton with her finger to her lips, shushing everyone who passes by, even when we're not making noise. And if you do raise your voice to anything above a whisper, she'll call the police at the drop of a hat."

"But why?"

"I don't really know. That's just the way things have always been. But shush up and listen. I'm almost done. Beatrice Bathwater has tissues up her cardigan sleeve that have been there since the Second World War. She's a manager at the factory, and she's head of the tourism board. Her job is to make sure all of England knows how very lovely and special Thumpton is. She makes sure people from all over the country pour into our little town on market mornings to buy handmade napkins and tablecloths and whatever other nonsense we can pawn off. And every Monday night, she walks all over the square, taking a toothbrush to the bricks."

"A toothbrush?"

"She brushes them—between the bricks, over the bricks, around the doorways, until they sparkle like rows of white teeth."

"But . . . *why*?"

"They like their history, those P's and Q's. They want to make sure this town looks just like it did in the 1500s."

"Didn't English people throw their poop out their windows in the 1500s?"

Jeevan considered this. "You know when you get a postcard in the post? And you think, *That place can't possibly look like that in real life?* Well, that's what Beatrice Bathwater wants Thumpton to look like. In real life. Every sodding day."

"But she can't fix the apostrophes."

"Would you leave off about the apostrophes?" He takes a big bite of ice cream and speaks with his mouth full, cream dripping down his chin. "Mum doesn't think much of her, down at the factory."

"What does she do there?"

"At the factory? She sews the little flowers on to the table-cloths and the poncy little serviettes and the snot-rags. It's all Asians, working there. That's why there're so many of us here. Why else would we live in Thumpton-on-Soar? Who else would make the stuff for market?"

"I thought the market was a thing where farmers brought their vegetables and animals, and spice traders brought their spices. That's what you—" I caught myself. "That's what someone told me."

"Oh, well. That's how it used to be. That's what Thumpton's famous for. But now, they just make things in a factory for tourists. Thumpton pretends to be this perfect little historical English town, int'it? But really, all the precious Englishness is made by Asians." This made him laugh. "No one mentions that bit, do they?"

He gazed into the distance for a while. The wind picked up and blew along the square, sending the signs creaking on their hinges.

"Anyway," he said. "That's the Peace and Quiet Commission. The you-know-whos. Best mind your P's and Q's."

TRACK 9
And She Was

Archie Gopalan was trouble. Her brother knew it. Her mother knew it. All of Alphabet Street knew it. Whether she was winning candy-spitting competitions off the canal bridge or sprinting through Thumpton's market square, she lived her life on the verge of a scolding, a ticket, a royal telling-off, or worse. She was a shrieking dervish of a girl, a big swollen zit on the face of her perfect postcard town, a terrible example to young people everywhere. To me, she was magnificent.

I hadn't met Archie yet, as Jeevan and I sat in the market square eating our ice cream and riffling through his bag of sweets. When I looked up, I realized he'd been staring at me. "Why aren't you talking?" he asked.

"What do you mean?"

"You've gone quiet. It's giving me the creeps. Like you're plotting something."

I frowned. "I'm not plotting anything." I realized Jeevan was still freaked out about me. I mean, I couldn't really blame him. I was thinking about the twitching curtains on Alphabet Street, the people who crept around this town like church mice, skittering indoors at the slightest sign of commotion.

Just then, Disco Baba's truck trundled by, its speakers *boom-hiss*ing. When he spotted us, Disco Baba stuck his head out the window. "Jeevan, my boy! On the bridge!"

Jeevan looked up, uninterested, and shrugged.

"Stop her! Before they find her!"

"Okay," Jeevan grumbled. The sun had come out. Jeevan got to his feet and stretched, drinking in its warmth. He didn't seem all that bothered about Archie.

"Where is she?" I asked. "Where's your sister?"

As if to answer my question, I heard a shout from the bridge. A group of teenagers stood in the middle of it. One stood taller than the others. It was her.

A tiny alarm rang in my head. My vision wobbled. *Deepest sympathies.* The little card with the flowers. The black box on the computer screen. The aunt who haunted the corners of my world. Here she was, as real as the hair on my head. As solid as the stones beneath my feet. The air around her seemed to shimmer and tremble. Archie Aunty.

Archie Aunty balanced on the edge of the bridge. A teenage boy held her by the legs as she wibbled and wobbled, trying to keep her balance. Just within her reach hung one of the town's signs.

"Leave it to my numpty of a sister to be balancing on the edge of a bridge and shouting like a harpy. She probably thinks no one can see her."

His numpty of a sister had brown skin, big eyes lined thickly in black, lips that sparkled and spangled in the sunlight, an explosion of a ponytail shooting off one side of her head. She wore a striped T-shirt and a thousand bracelets. She wore lace fingerless gloves and leg warmers over her jeans.

The four others, brown like us, were about fifteen or sixteen. One of them had brought a boombox that thumped and rattled at their feet, sending music trailing over the canal. I'd never seen teenagers like this, rough and squawky, lumpy around the edges, like loaves of unbaked bread. I thought of the teenagers at Academie Fontaine, the ones who danced for the Studio Company. I'd spent years watching them from a distance, catching glimpses of them stretching at the barre or wrapping their toes in tape, their legs veined and muscular, their feet as wide and gnarled as the roots of an oak tree. For as long as I could remember, I'd wanted to be one of those strange, magical creatures.

"Oy, piss off back home, you little spod!" the girl snarled. She was looking straight at us.

Jeevan cupped his hands around his mouth. "I see you, Archie Gopalan! You said you'd be at the library!" Balancing his ice cream cone, he charged at the bridge. I ran after him.

As we got nearer, I saw a fat red felt-tip pen in her hand. The poster she'd been drawing on was stark white with black lettering. It had started off looking like this:

ABSOLUTELY
POSITIVELY
NO STREET PLAY OR LOITERING
PLEASE KEEP
THUMPTON-ON-SOAR
A QUIET TOWN FOR QUIET PEOPLE
PEACE ORDINANCE STRICTLY ENFORCED

But after Archie had had her way with it, the poster looked like this:

ABSOLUTELY
POSITIVELY
NO STREET PLAY OR LOITERING
PLEASE KEEP
THUMPTON-ON-SOAR
A QUIET TOWN FOR QUIET PEOPLE
PEACE ORDINANCE STRICTLY ENFORCED

GET STUFFED

Word of the sign must have traveled, quick as a shout, along the canal and into town, because already, a group of people was approaching the bridge. While Archie's group was young and brown, and jumped and spat like hot oil, this group was quiet, old, white-haired, white-skinned, all cardigans and stiff collars and pearls. It was them. The you-know-whos. The P's and Q's. They moved steadily toward the bridge, straight for Archie's group. On either side of them walked a police officer, each in a domed black hat, batons swinging from their hands.

"Oh, bad. This is bad," Jeevan muttered. "They're coming to get her."

"What? What do you mean?"

"That's them. Winterbottom and Bathwater and Ginger Biscuits. They've got the police and they're taking her away. She's already had her last warning—Archie!" he shouted. "Archie, get out of here! Run!"

Archie's head snapped up. Even from a distance, I could see her brace, like a deer ready to bolt.

Just then, very faintly, a *boom–hiss*. It grew louder. *Boom–hiss–hiss. Boom–hiss.* Disco Baba. He was coming up faster and faster, speeding toward us from the other side of the bridge. This time, something was different about his truck. What was it? I stared at it as it drew closer, its big whipped cone sprouting from its roof. The music was getting louder as it hurtled toward the bridge. The teenagers turned to watch, too. The P's and Q's and the police with their batons stopped in their tracks.

"Why's he going so fast?" Jeevan asked.

"That's it!" I said. "Ice cream trucks go slow. This one's going fast. But why?"

"And the music—"

"It's *loud*." The music was cranked up to top volume, scraping against the speakers, a staticky mess of drumbeats and synthesizers and a woman's high, strong melody.

The ice cream truck flew past the teenagers. Archie clung

to a pole. Her friends pressed themselves against the side of the bridge. They took one look at the speeding truck and scattered. Disco Baba flew past them, still blaring music, probably breaking every law Thumpton had to offer. From the side of the bridge, Mr. Winterbottom raised his cane.

"After him!" he shouted.

The policemen just looked at each other, bewildered.

"I said after him!" Mr. Winterbottom cried, almost screamed. The bobbies ran after the truck and the P's and Q's followed at a heated crawl. Only one, a plump lady with red hair, hung behind.

She made her way onto the bridge. She wasn't afraid of the teenagers. She just stood beneath them, crossed her arms, and peered up at them. "Pack it in, you lot," she said. "He may not be here to rescue you next time."

Archie watched thoughtfully as the ice cream truck disappeared across the square, the police running after it. So that's what Disco Baba's sprint across the bridge was all about: He'd been creating a diversion. The only thing louder and more rule-breaking than Archie Gopalan was a high-speed, disco-blasting ice cream truck. Carefully, she lowered herself to sit on the ledge of the bridge. From her pocket, she drew a pink-and-white-striped bag, just like ours, fished a red candy from it, and popped it into her mouth.

Jeevan turned and began to walk away. "Let's get out of here." He grabbed my sleeve and pulled me back the way we came.

"Why?"

From the bridge, the tallest boy called out. "Oy, Jeeves! Where you off to?"

"Who's that?" I asked.

"That's Chuzzy. Let's go back the other way."

"What's his problem?"

"Come on, Boomi—"

Chuzzy again: "Jeev-oh, don't be frightened! The blue meanies are gone!" His words were kind but the way he said them wasn't. Chuzzy had a sour edge to him that made my teeth ache. Archie didn't say anything or try to stop him. She just sat on the bridge, ripped the head off a Swedish fish, and scowled into the distance.

Then, out of nowhere, she seemed to wake up. She looked over at us, then peered at me. My heart quickened. Then she shouted, "Jeev-oh—Jimmy!" She turned to her friends. "Calls himself Jimmy now. Oy, Jimmy! Who's your little friend there? Did you find a new mate?"

The others laughed and joined in. "Jimmy! Come back! Who's your mate?"

Jeevan turned and walked away from the bridge. "Idiots," he muttered. "They're going to get in trouble. Let's take another bridge."

"I think they're just fooling around—"

"I know another way," he insisted, pulling at my elbow.

"I want to meet your sister—"

Thump! Jeevan closed his eyes. He took a deep breath

and kept walking, away from Archie, away from the bridge. Another thump. A hard candy landed on the pavement at my feet. "They're throwing candy at us?" I wouldn't have believed it if a bullet of butterscotch hadn't, just then, hit my calf.

Jeevan touched the back of his head, where the first candy had hit. A red peppermint bounced off his shoulder. "Keep walking," he said.

"But you can't just—"

"Keep walking. We just have to get out of here." A lemon drop hit his shoulder, and the boys shouted and guffawed. When I turned to face them, a hard pink sweet nailed me right in the forehead.

"Um. Ex-*cuse me*?" I growled.

"Boomi. No—"

I stomped over to the bridge, my ears ringing. No one treated Dad that way. No one treated *me* that way. Archie hopped up onto the ledge of the bridge and squatted there like a jungle cat ready to pounce. I walked right up to her, like I'd known her all my life, like I wasn't terrified at that moment, like I wasn't half considering jumping off the bridge and swimming away.

I looked into Archie's eyes—my eyes—and I said, "You can't do that."

Howls and guffaws from the group. "Ooooh, madam!" Archie cooed. "I do beg your pardon!"

I turned to look at Jeevan, who had walked up to stand with me. Behind his enormous glasses, he looked helpless.

I took a step closer to Archie. "Why did you do that to him?"

"Well, don't you talk funny," Archie said. She leaned in, a mocking glint in her eye. "You're American, int'it? Say what you just said."

Fireworks of rage popped behind my eyes, and all I could see were explosions of light. I could almost feel lightning zapping out from my ears. "I said, *Why did you do that to him?*"

From her perch on the bridge, Archie grinned at me, her face close to mine. Before I could duck or move, she reached into her pocket, pulled out a hard candy, and flicked it right at my face. It hit me in the nose. That was it. Everything came rushing back: Dad's memorial; the sad bunch of flowers; the dumb, boring Christmas cards; the big Aunty-shaped hole that hung black and empty in our house; and now this. It was too much. I lunged forward and shoved Archie in the chest. And I watched, like I was watching a movie, as she reeled backward, her arms spinning in great circles, as she lost her balance and toppled off the bridge, and down, down, down into the gray-green waters of the canal.

I stood, frozen. Jeevan stood frozen, his mouth wide open. The rest of the teenagers stood frozen, too, all of us watching Archie thrashing at the water, pointing up at me and growling with rage, her candies floating around her like a dozen rainbow-colored little sailboats.

Jeevan shouted to me, "Boomi, run!" I sprinted back the way we'd come. Archie climbed out of the water, dripping and furious. I could hear shouts behind us, a stampede of feet as the gang from the bridge drew closer. "Faster!" Jeevan shouted. When he reached the edge of the bridge, he jumped down the three stone steps that led to the street, then toward the square. I ran across the bridge, harder than I've ever run, my knees flying out in front of me, the thunder of eight feet behind me.

I jumped from the top step. Just as I landed, Jeevan turned to me and froze like a photograph. Uh-oh. Around me, the colors of the world faded to yellows and golds. I hovered in the air, and then, out of nowhere, came a blinding flash. Followed by a BOOM. Soft light. Silence. Nothing.

TRACK 10
Break My Stride

With a crash, I landed on the floor of my own room. It took me a few seconds to know where I was, when I was, who I was. I looked up and saw the yellow boombox. I remembered. But I didn't understand. What made me flash back to the present? And how?

My stomach jolted with pain. My insides twisted and I doubled over, moaning. My hands shook. So did my feet. I did not feel good. Not at all.

A loud knock and the door opened. Mom stomped in. I shoved the boombox under my bed and jumped under the covers, my arms and legs still glowing. As my eyes regained their focus, I could see that it was morning. Mom stood before me in her bathrobe, little foil wrappers spilling from her fingers. The chocolate bars.

I moaned some more. My stomach really hurt. Maybe she'd feel sorry for me.

"Oh, I see," Mom said. "We've got a sore tummy, have

we?" She sprinkled the chocolate wrappers on the floor. "It's no wonder, the number of chocolates you ate last night."

I rolled to sitting and squinted at the wrappers. "It's not that many."

"Not that many?" Mom got down on her knees. She reached into her robe pocket and pulled out the whole jumbo plastic bag, filled with empty wrappers. "What do you call this, then?" She dumped the wrappers onto the carpet. "Did you eat this all last night? By your*self*? Were you hiding food from me? Is this what we've come to? Do you care at all about your body? Do you care about ballet? Have all those years gone to waste?" She kept asking questions. I couldn't answer any of them.

When she sat on my bed, her legs barely touched the floor. Her heel kept almost kicking the boombox. "I got a call this morning," she said. "They're still deciding if you get a second audition. If you do and you pass, you'll be on probation. They'll watch you for a month and decide if you get to stay. And if you do well during the probationary period, you'll be admitted to the Studio Company." She looked intently into my eyes. "They *never* do this, Boomi. You've got to get in shape, practice your audition routine, and get your act together. Do you understand me?"

I nodded.

She softened a little. "Don't you want to be in the dance school, Boomi? Like Bebe is? Don't you want to be with Bebe?"

Something inside me crumbled when she said that. "No," I muttered.

71

"No?"

"Bebe's not my friend anymore, Mom."

"What? Why not?"

"Didn't you notice?"

She just stared back at me.

"Didn't you notice that we stopped our online dance things? And she never messages me? Did you notice *anything* about me this year?"

Mom considered this for a few seconds. "It's been a hard year for all of us."

"Not for Bebe. She just got more popular. She somehow got *more* friends during the pandemic. So many that she didn't need me."

"I'm sure that's not the case, darling."

I slumped down on the bed next to her. "She wouldn't talk to me at auditions this weekend. She made me feel . . . dumb." I looked at Mom, who blinked back at me. I don't think she knew what to say.

"Well. Maybe if you get back into the dance school, Bebe will be your friend again." I'm no psychologist, but I'm pretty sure that was the wrong thing to say. "Now, let's weigh you before you shower."

I stood on the scale she'd brought in. Instead of looking at the number, I stared at myself in the mirror. In its reflection, I could see Mom write down the number. It wasn't a good number. She shook her head.

When I was little, if I ever had a tummy ache, Mom would

have me lie on my front and she'd stroke my back. It always helped. This time, I closed the door behind her and flopped facedown on my bed, thinking about Thumpton and Jeevan and Archie and the bridge. I was dying to tell someone about it all. I couldn't tell Mom, obviously. Normally, I'd tell Bebe. Now I just had myself. How did I flash into 1986? And how the heck did I flash back? That was the most surprising part, flashing back when I jumped off the bridge.

I took a long, hot shower and started to feel better. When I got out, Mom was in my room again, a new smile on her face, a long strip of paper looped around her fingers. Measuring tape. "Measurements are more accurate than weight," she said sunnily.

"Measurements for what?"

She released the folds of the measuring tape, and it dangled to the ground like a snake. "So we know how big you are, Boomi, and how much you're losing."

"Oh, come on! Are you for real right now?" Mom didn't answer. She just pulled me to her and wrapped the measuring tape around one arm, then the other. She wrote numbers down in a little book. I winced when the tape cut into my stomach. "Remember Olga Petrov?" Mom asked, kneeling to measure my thighs. Olga Petrov was the ballerina from *The Nutcracker*. "She's got the perfect body for ballet. She's as light as a whisper. That's what we're going for. Think *whisper*." I looked down at her. She gave me a reassuring smile. She was hopeful. Could she not see my body? I wasn't made of feathers and whispers, I boomed like thunder. It was even in my name. Boomi. BOOM!

Mom got to her feet. "Come have your breakfast," she said. When she left, I turned to my computer and typed in *probationary definition*. It didn't make me feel better.

In the kitchen, my usual row of cereal boxes had vanished. Cocoa Puffs, gone. Honey Smacks, gone. Apple Jacks, not a trace. Mom plunked half a grapefruit on the table, along with a plate of quivering egg whites and one lonely unbuttered piece of toast. She sat down next to me and looked deep into my eyes, like she was waiting for me to talk.

"I looked up probationary," I said. "It means *the release of an offender from detention*."

She sighed. "And?"

"So why am I on probation at Fontaine? Did I *offend* someone?"

"There are other definitions for probation, Boom. It's also a trial period, a length of time for you to prove yourself."

"To prove what?"

"To prove that you're willing to work hard—"

"I do work hard."

"—and lose a little weight."

"I'm not that fat, Mom."

"I know that."

"I'm totally average compared to almost every kid at school." This was absolutely not true. But Mom accepted it.

She smoothed down my hair. "You have such a gift. So

74

much presence. So much potential."

Potential. Do you know what potential is? Potential is a long, bony finger pointing to everything about you that's not good enough. It's what you *could* be if you tried. Would you rather have a lot of potential, or know that everyone loves you just as you are? All I wanted, at that moment, was to be all right, just the way I was. I looked at my mom. That day, she wore peacock feather earrings that swayed daintily around her slim little neck. She had no idea how it felt to look like me, to carry all this body around, all this thunder.

"Mom."

"Yes?"

"Were you fat when you were my age?"

She looked uncomfortable. "No. Not really. I guess I was skinny."

"Freakishly skinny?"

"What? No."

"Did you have a lot of friends?"

"I suppose so."

"Did boys like you?"

"I think they probably did. Why are you asking me that?"

"I don't think I'm like you. I don't think I ever *will* be like you."

Mom didn't say anything for a while. I could see she was trying to figure out the right thing to say, the thing that would get me to focus on my diet, on my body, on my life as a dancer. Then she leaned forward and placed a hand on mine. I could see that she meant to do the right thing. She really did. "It wasn't easy growing up back there." *Back there* was England. "We had a hard time, me and Dad. All us Asian kids. Being Asian—it did us no favors back then. But *here*, Boomi . . ." *Here* was San Francisco. "*Here* isn't exactly perfect. But it's certainly better than it was for me. You don't have to worry so much about being brown."

"Just about being fat," I said.

Mom pulled her hand from mine. I'd gone too far. I could see her closing up again. She fiddled with her wedding ring, which she still wore. She wouldn't look at me. "I just want the best for you." She started to get up.

"Okay," I said abruptly.

She froze, half standing. "Okay what?"

"Okay, I'll try to lose weight. And I'll audition again, if they let me."

Mom nodded. "That would make me very happy."

Would you rather make yourself happy or your mom? That morning, I chose my mom. I didn't know what that would mean for me.

After breakfast, I went downstairs. Normally, I'd scrounge up some pocket change and take it to the donut shop. The donut shop around the corner has all kinds of donuts you wouldn't expect—donuts with marshmallows, donuts with bacon, even candy cane donuts. But no bacon donuts today. I was going be a whisper, and the road to whisperdom was not paved with donuts. And besides, the chocolates from last night still burbled in my stomach.

I looked out my window. On the sidewalk, Denny sat in his usual spot. A knot in my tummy loosened. I went downstairs and out the door.

Today, Denny sat smiling with his eyes closed, slathering his face with sun. July in San Francisco doesn't promise any kind of summer, but today was almost hot. When he heard me, Denny opened his eyes. "What's the word, Boomi-girl? Heading to the donut shop? Pick me up a maple glaze?"

"I don't think so, Denny. I might be tempted to get myself one."

"I don't see what's wrong with that." He squinted up at me. "You on a diet or something?"

"I guess so."

"Well, that's a stinkin' idea if I ever heard one."

"I'm losing weight for dance. I'm re-auditioning in a few weeks, to try to get in. They already rejected me, but they might let me in if I've really changed."

"Changed. You want to change?"

I shrugged.

"Bull honkey."

"What?"

"Well, first off, to heck with 'em for rejecting you. And second, why would you want to change? Can't you just be *you*? Embrace the boom, Boomi! You're big and beautiful and you should be proud!"

I smiled a little. I gave him a small wave and started to walk off.

"Try out that boombox yet?" he asked. "Any good?"

I screeched to a halt. Of course! I could tell Denny! I turned back. "Denny," I said. "Can I tell you something? Something important?"

"Always."

I crouched down next to him. "Denny, this thing happened. It was the craziest thing that's ever happened to me." I told him everything—how the boombox popped around my room like a toaster, the flash of light, landing in my dad's room, the candy store, the bridge, and the flash back through time and space. He listened to all of this with total calm. When I finished, he ran his hand through his beard. "Huh. That's interesting," he said, like I'd just told him it was going to rain. "Are you going back?"

"Back to 1986?" The question, I realized, had been lurking in my mind, waiting for me to notice it. "I sort of ditched my dad—I left him being chased by his sister, who was furious. I'd pushed her into the canal."

"Sounds to me like you should probably go see about that." The thing I loved about Denny was that you could tell him anything—*anything*—and he'd act like it was totally normal.

"You're right." I thought about the boombox, waiting beneath my bed. "I don't really know how, though . . . and what if I can't get back here again?"

"It's a gamble. Did your mom notice you missing?"

"No."

"But if your mom had been standing there when you flashed to the past, would she have seen it happen?"

"Yeah. I think?"

"And time was passing over here, while you were over there."

"Right. But more slowly, I think."

"So, you entered some kinda distortion in the space-time continuum. A day over there isn't as long as a day over here."

"I don't know. Yes? Probably." My head hurt. "You're scrambling my brain, Denny."

"Welcome to my world, cupcake."

Sometimes, when things got confusing or sad or just too big, I'd choose a memory of Dad and go over it and over it, rubbing at it like a lucky stone. Here's one of my favorites: I must have been nine or ten. Dad sat against my bedroom wall.

"Thumpton-on-Soar, Boomi, was a dour and sour little town. It sat smack in the middle of Leicestershire, which sat smack in the middle of England. And in my mind, Thumpton-on-Soar, that dour and sour little town, sat *smack* at the center of the universe.

"Our little brick house looked like every other little brick house on Alphabet Street."

"And did Thumpton-on-Soar look like every other town in England?"

"No," he said immediately. "No, it did not. Thumpton was

79

an old market town, you know. That means that hundreds of years ago, people would come from all around to trade their wares—their vegetables, their animals, their spices from the Far East. And the town square still looks as it did all those hundreds of years ago. The locals have made sure of that. It still has the old cobblestone streets, the stone bridges over its canals. The buildings on the old town square were built in the 1500s. Not that I cared a jot about all that, growing up. To me, Thumpton was just a pokey, dreary old town, where every face you met was as worn and gray as the cobblestones." He paused for a few seconds, thinking. "But on a sunny summer's day, Thumpton-on-Soar shone like a pearl. And the parties we'd have! Dancing till we dropped on Diwali. Partying till we popped on Pongal."

"Dad."

"It's true."

"Why did you leave? Why did you never go back?"

"Things changed, Pickle. The town changed. And I have Paati here, don't I?"

"But what about your sister? She lives there, doesn't she?" I'd thought of the girl in the photograph, the girl no one talked about. Two braids and a dimple, her nose sharp and her smile wide, just like Dad's.

"No. She lives in London. And travels for work."

"If she travels for work, she could travel here to see us. Couldn't she?"

Dad shifted in his seat, out of the moonlight and into the dark. "It's late," he said. "Time to close those big brown eyes."

Bedtimes are a parent's quickest escape route. The second you ask a question they don't want to answer, it's time to close your big brown eyes.

All morning, I thought about my conversation with Denny. Something had been poking at me since he'd given me the boombox. From behind Mom's office door, her cello climbed up a scale and down. I padded into the living room and opened our board game cupboard. I shoved aside Monopoly and Boggle and pulled out Dad's junk box. It was an old tin, mottled with rust, *Tetley Tea Bags* printed on the lid, dark blue with a gold-white border. Back in my room, I pried it open and sifted through Dad's things: an old white handkerchief, a report card that I'd read through a hundred times. *Jeevan is an exemplary student, quiet and well-behaved. Exceptional effort in maths and French.* With it was an old diagram he'd drawn on graph paper, folded into a small square, stiff with age. He'd titled it in clear, bold handwriting: *The comparative velocities of boiled sweets.* I smiled. This old diagram finally made sense. Below it I'd added my own stash—stupid things, mostly. Like a knotted, tangled old yo-yo. A plastic egg filled with putty. A Boba Dreams customer loyalty card with just one stamp left to go.

At the very bottom of the tin, I found what I was looking for. A plastic case, with a paper insert folded into it. It had been there for as long as we'd owned the box, but I'd never given it much thought. *Radio Mix One*, it read. I knew I'd seen those words before! On the main flap was a list of songs. The first, written in Dad's careful hand, "Jump (For My Love)." That was the song that had sent me to Thumpton. The second was "Rebel Yell."

"Dad made this," I whispered. A shadow flopped down next to me. *Oooh, what's Dad made? Is he coming back, then?*

"Get lost, Shadow."

Now, sitting in my room, listening to the moan of Mom's cello, I decided Denny was right. I had to go see about Jeevan. I pulled out the boombox. It seemed to have snuck under my bed. With my fingernail, I scraped away some of the grime, revealing the smooth yellow surface beneath. I could still smell the candy shop, could feel the just-before-lightning buzz of the air. What if it had all been a strange and vivid dream? The kind that used to make me talk in my sleep when I was little? There was only one way to find out.

I pressed play. Again, nothing. And then, the tiniest click. I looked down to see the wheels of the player spinning, slow and steady. A hushing sound, like radio static, filled the room. Then, at last, a keyboard, electronic and bare. Its notes climbed and fell. A heavy drumbeat. The music swelled. "Rebel Yell." I turned the volume down, but the music only got louder. A man's voice started up, tough and spiky, like barbed wire. The boombox started to shake. And then it jumped. It jumped again. It popped off the carpet and onto its back, still wriggling and jiggling. Beneath it, a pool of light began to grow.

You know what happened next.

A puddle of light. BOOM. Silence.

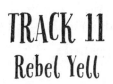

TRACK 11
Rebel Yell

I landed—*whomp!*—on hard pavement, surrounded by plain brick houses all smashed together. My head felt like it was on fire, and when I touched my hair, it was hot. Sparks of light sizzled on my arms. I looked ahead and saw Archie, hunched over, dripping wet, staring at me. Her friends stood around her, their mouths dropped open and eyes bulging, like a bunch of fish out of water.

Taking a chance, I raised my hands above my head, like a monster from a storybook, and let out a long, savage, beastly ROAR. Then I sprinted straight at them.

"Run!" Archie squealed. The group—everyone but Jeevan—bolted. I ran after them, my arms flailing, and let out my own rebel yell. They ran faster, around the corner, out of sight.

With the coast clear and the street quiet, I could hear the boombox they'd left behind on the bridge. It was playing the same song I'd played back in my room. Jeevan jogged over to meet me.

"That song," I said, pointing to the radio. The song was some kind of portal. I was traveling through music. "That song is how I got here!"

Jeevan put his hands on his hips and stared me down. "You have got some explaining to do."

"So, let me get this straight," Jeevan said, his face scrunched with concentration. We sat on the steps to the bridge. "You know me. In the future. Are we friends?"

I shrugged.

His eyes widened. "God, we're not, like, *married*, are we?"

"Ew! No! That doesn't even make sense! Look, I can't tell you how I know you. You'll find out eventually, anyway."

"What *can* you tell me?"

Sitting on the bridge, the streets quiet around us, I told him everything I could. I told him that I was from the year 2021. That I traveled here through a boombox. That time-traveling boomboxes were *not* a common thing in the year 2021. And that no, we didn't have flying cars or robot butlers. I told him about the tape, Radio Mix One. I told him how it felt to flash back—the hot, sick feeling in my stomach, like my insides were unfolding. The pool of light, the sizzle and glow after I landed. But I didn't tell him about Mom or Paati or even Denny. Jeevan sat on the curb and gazed at me, thinking, for a long time. And then he said, "Explain it all again, please."

So, I said it all again and didn't add anything. Television

had taught me exactly three things about time travel. Number one: Keep it low-pro. Don't let people see you appear and disappear. I was clearly failing at number one. Number two: Try not to run into your past self. If your past self sees your present self, both your brains could melt. Number three: Don't warn people about things or try to change the course of history. The results could be disastrous.

"All right," Jeevan said. "So really, you're a bit like Doctor Who."

"Doctor who?"

"Yes."

"No," I said. "Doctor *who*?"

"Yes, Doctor Who."

I squeezed my head between my palms. Is this what Denny felt like every day? "But—*who*?"

"*Doctor Who*." He stared at me. I stared at him. "Let's change the subject."

"Okay."

"How do I know you're not a scam artist?" he asked.

"Ask me something only you would know."

"Who's my favorite band?"

"Queen."

"They're not."

"They will be."

"Look," he said, "all I know is that one minute, I was being pelted with boiled sweets, and the next minute, the world flashed like lightning, and you were gone."

"You'll just have to believe me." I shrugged.

"Tell me something else, then. Something you know about me."

I thought about Dad, all the weird little details of his existence. "You hate snorting sounds, like the kind pigs make," I said, "which is ironic, because you snore like a warthog." He sat back, listening. "You sleep with a pillow over your head and earplugs in your ears. You hate heavy blankets. You hate being too warm. You love chocolate with almonds, and you think cookies with raisins are a cruel prank. You always wanted a dog, but your mom wouldn't get you one because she thought they smelled. You like swimming but you hate getting your feet wet. Okra makes you gag."

"What will I be when I grow up?"

My dad, I wanted to say. "What do you want to be?"

"That's not what I asked."

We stared at each other for a second. "Who are you?" he asked. "How do you know me?"

I thought about telling him. If he knew he was my dad, would he let me hug him?

"No!" he cried. "Wait! Don't tell me! Revealing anything about my future could bugger up the course of human existence!"

I scowled at him. "Are you mansplaining time travel to me?"

"Am I what?"

"I'm the one who just *did* the time travel. Look, I won't tell

86

you anything more than I already have. Believe me, you don't want to know."

He looked worried. "I don't want to know what?"

I thought about all the things he didn't know. I could tell him about boba. I could tell him about TikTok. I could tell him about the internet! I could tell him about—about— My mind slowed to a halt, like someone had thrown cement in its gears. I tried to push it forward. This was my chance, my chance to really make a difference in our lives, but I couldn't think how. I opened my mouth and heard the weak trickle of my own voice.

"Do you know about boba?"

"Who?" He looked bewildered. "Boomi. You can't tell me anything. Even if you think it'll make me the richest person on the planet. Even if you think it'll save—I don't know— *Boba*, whoever that is."

We stared at each other, the possibilities gathering like storm clouds. Jeevan shook his head. "I mean it," he whispered. "Not a word."

I hugged my knees. "Okay."

We sat like that for a few quiet minutes, until finally, he spoke. "This is all very weird," he said.

"I know."

A few minutes later, we were back on Alphabet Street. Disco Baba had parked his truck across the street. He climbed down off the passenger seat, pulled a bunch of keys from his chest pocket, and walked up the steps to his front door.

"Who were those boys with Archie?"

"Local lads," Jeevan said. "They know my sister and they get a rise out of making me miserable."

"I could tell."

"They were being positively angelic today, compared to the usual."

"Do they always throw candies at you?"

"Not always. Rocks, sometimes. Or snow, if there is any. Whatever's at hand, really. But sweets are the worst. Kola Kubes, especially—they've got the highest velocity. Lemon sherbets are pretty bad, too. Now that everyone's eating jelly sweets, it's gotten a bit better. The jellies don't hit as hard."

I wanted to ask why they threw candies at him, why his sister let her friends bully him like that, but I saw the hunch of his shoulders, the way he kicked at the pavement as he walked, and I decided to let the question drop.

We neared his house. "The window's still open!" He ran ahead of me and hitched himself onto the windowsill. I caught up with him just as his head and shoulders disappeared into the room. He wriggled farther in, until only his feet and legs stuck out on to the street. "Give us a push, will you?" I grabbed his shins and shoved him forward.

"One more shove."

I shoved. He fell with a thud to his bedroom floor. A second later, his head popped up. "Bugger," he said.

"What?"

"We should have put you through first. Can you manage?"

"You've obviously never met a dancer," I said, trying to hoist myself onto the windowsill. It was harder than it looked. I grunted and strained. Did time travel make me weaker? I tried not to let on how hard this was. "My dance teacher? She says that if you want your body to do something, you just call the right muscles and tell them to get to work." I managed to hoist myself up, finally, my waist teetering against the windowsill.

And then, from behind me, a voice: "I reckon the front door's easiest."

I turned: It was Archie, her arms crossed, her head cocked to the side, her ponytail swaying in the breeze. As I twisted around even more, I lost my balance. My upper body tipped over the windowsill and I went spilling over the ledge but caught myself, my arms wheeling wildly in the air.

"Oh, lovely," Jeevan said. "Dead graceful. I can see that you're a dancer." He was fiddling with his boombox, dialing into a radio station.

"Your sister!" I said.

"What's she want?"

I scraped myself up as fast as I could and looked back out the window. But Archie was gone.

Just then, the bedroom door flew open. Archie stood in the doorway, her eyes wide. She walked over to me and, with one finger, reached out and prodded my shoulder.

ZAP! A crackle of electricity shot between us. She jumped

back and stared at me like I'd shot her with an alien death-ray.

"No," I said. "That was just a regular shock—" It was nothing more than the tiny jolt that happens, now and then, when you touch someone. Right?

"You," she said, her voice low and throaty. "Who are you?"

"I'm Boomi."

Slowly, she stalked a circle around me. She peered at my arms, where the faintest sheen of light still fizzled and sparked. "It's like . . . it's like you're made of lightning," she said. She peered into my face. "The lightning child." Her eyes widened dramatically. "The lightning child of Alphabet Street."

I turned to Jeevan, who was watching her nervously, as clueless as I was about what to do next. The radio tinned behind us, a commercial for cat food. Archie straightened up, a slow smile spreading across her face. "Mum's gonna flip when she hears about this!" Her smile broke into a grin and she turned and ran out of the room.

"Archie! No!" Jeevan shouted. He ran after her.

"What's she doing?" I called. "She can't tell anyone—"

But he'd run off and left me in his empty room. I could hear Archie stomping through the house. She might have been telling her mom. I thought of Paati finding me. How would I explain myself? What would it be like to see her here, now? I was throttled by a sudden urge to get the heck out of there.

The window. My only escape. I slung one leg over the sill and half hoisted myself up. Then I wobbled, lost my grip, and crashed back down to Jeevan's floor. Jeevan opened the door and lunged at me, Archie just behind him.

But then the world stopped. Jeevan froze, his hand raised, his mouth open. The room went silent and perfectly still, except for the song on the boombox, a jaunty keyboard and a man's deep, reedy voice. The music swelled. The carpet flooded with light. A flash. A boom. And I was gone.

TRACK 12
Safety Dance

This time, the landing was brutal—flat on my back with a crash that knocked the wind out of me. I rolled around on the carpet for a while, my stomach twisting, my back shrieking, my eyes squeezed shut. After a few minutes, the pain subsided. I examined my arm, where the sparks of light were starting to dim. I took a deep breath. I'd never been so glad to see my room.

"Boomi."

I shot up. There sat Bebe Jacobs, her mouth squeezed shut, her cheeks puffed out in utter amazement. Her breath whooshed in and out of her nostrils.

"Hi," I said, catching my own breath, trying to calm the tilt and whirl of the room around me. Under my bed, the boombox played the same song Jeevan's boombox had been playing.

She spoke carefully, quietly. "What *was* that?"

"Um . . . what was what?"

Her eyes flitted around the room, which looked mostly

normal, except for the rapidly shrinking pool of light by my dresser.

"Power outage," I lied. "How'd you get in here?"

She stared at me, like she didn't believe a word that came out of me. "Your mom called me."

"Oh." My cheeks grew hot with embarrassment. "Sorry."

"What's going on with you? What just happened? You weren't here and then—and then—"

"And then you heard a boom and saw a flash of light and then I fell from nowhere and I was glowing?"

She nodded slowly.

"It's a long story." Another time, another year, I would have told her everything. But now, today, Bebe felt like a stranger. I'd forgotten how to talk to her. I *wanted* to tell her everything that had happened. I just . . . couldn't.

"Your mom said she was worried about you," Bebe said, tucking her feet under her. "I kind of get why. Now."

Could Mom have known about the time travel? About the boombox? It sat quietly under my bed. No one had touched it.

"She asked me why we stopped being friends," Bebe continued. "Is that what you told her? That we stopped being friends?"

"Well, we did. Didn't we?"

She picked at the carpet.

I took a deep breath, gathering up my courage. "You basically ignored me at auditions," I said. I waited for her to deny this, to explain, to tell me I was wrong. She didn't. She just kept listening. That made me a little braver. "And before that, you stopped Zooming with me. I thought—" My voice caught. But I forced myself to go on. "My dad died—" My voice screeched to a halt. If I said another word, I'd burst into tears.

We sat there, Bebe silent. "I knew your dad died." She went quiet again.

"Who were those girls at the audition? The ones you were standing with?"

"Oh—you know them. From fifth-grade dance camp, remember? We were in a pod together last fall. Amber, Sabine, and Cecily. Cece. We're Bebe and Cece." She grinned, then zapped her smile away. We used to be Bebe and Boomi. *This is it*, I thought. She was finally going to admit that she'd ended our friendship, that she'd abandoned me because I wasn't as old or cool or skinny as Cece and her crew. Because I embarrassed her. Because I was too much. Too big. Too pink-shoed, too smudge-kneed. Finally, she took a deep breath. *Here we go*, I thought.

"Your dad was really nice. I wish . . ." Bebe picked up her duffel bag and got to her feet. "I'm sorry."

I wanted to grab her by the shoulders and tell her I didn't need her to be sorry. I just needed her to be my friend.

"Wait—" I stood up. We weren't six anymore, and I couldn't just ask her to be my friend. How come when you get older, you get *worse* at asking for what you want?

"I have rehearsal," Bebe said, and turned to the door.

"No!"

She waited, her hand on the doorknob.

94

"I'm not mad at you. It's just . . . will you . . . ?" *Will you be my friend again?* But I couldn't say it. I flopped back down and managed not to cry, but I started to shake inside. Then I started to shake outside. I watched the tremble in my knees, my hands. An earthquake rumbled in my chest. Bebe dropped her bag to the floor and sat down with me. She put a hand on my knee and kept it there until the shaking stopped.

"Everything was horrible," I said at last.

"I know."

"I wished you were there."

She picked at the carpet. "I guess I was scared."

"Of what?"

"Talking to you. Or saying the wrong thing, I guess. I didn't know how you'd be after—after . . ." She trailed off.

"He died, Bebe. You can say it!"

"Okay. Okay. After he died. I was scared. And I'm a little scared now."

I wrapped my arms around myself and waited for her to say more.

"You had this huge thing happen to you, Boomi. This *huge* thing that only grown-ups have to deal with, normally. It felt like you were, I don't know, in another world."

"It did?" I'd never thought of it that way.

"I didn't know anything about your world. You were like an alien."

"Thanks," I mumbled. She didn't try to take it back. I guess she'd meant it. "So, you found new friends."

"Yeah. But that's all they are. New friends. You're still my oldest friend." She let out a trembling sigh. "I wasn't nice to you at auditions. I was trying to—" She hung her head, pinched at her tights. Then she looked back up at me. "You're my best friend."

"Even though I don't have a body like a whisper?" I asked.

"What?"

"A ballet body. Like a whisper. A light, thin body that hardly makes a sound."

She screwed up her face. "Where'd you get that from?"

"My mom. I think. Maybe she got it from a dance magazine or something—"

That's when Mom burst in. She didn't even knock this time. "Bebe, your mum's here. She asked me to hurry you along, love." We waited for Mom to close the door. Bebe turned to me.

"Earlier, with the light. You came out of nowhere. You have to tell me what happened," she said.

"Okay. Fine. I time traveled."

"What?"

"I traveled through time, into the past, and went back to the 1980s, when my dad was our age."

Her face went blank, like she'd turned off a light. "Fine. You don't have to tell me. But don't just make things up."

"I didn't!"

She sprang, silent as a cat, to her feet. "My mom's waiting," she said. Then she picked up her bag and left.

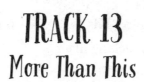

TRACK 13
More Than This

From my window, I watched Bebe walk out the front door and climb into her mom's SUV. My stomach knotted up tight and hard. I sifted through my memories for a good one, something to loosen that fist, but all that came up was this:

A couple weeks after our Boba Dreams trip, Dad's breathing got so bad that he had to go to the hospital. Since we weren't allowed to visit, we spoke to him through our laptop. He couldn't really speak very well. Words jumped from his mouth between breaths. "They're keeping me here"—*breath*—"for their own edification"—*breath*—"The nurses"—*breath*—"can't get"—*breath*— "enough of me." He grinned. I grinned back. I knew they were extra nice to Dad because he'd been a doctor there for almost twenty years. He'd brought a thousand babies into the world at that hospital.

One afternoon, I walked into the kitchen to find Mom on the laptop again. This time, tears streamed down her cheeks and her breath jumped in little hiccups. She straightened up and wiped at her face when she saw me. I heard Dad's voice. "She home?" Mom handed me the laptop, where his face filled the screen. Black stubble grew over his cheeks. His eyes were red, but he smiled. His voice was weak, and he breathed quickly, like he was sucking in air.

I turned to Mom. "What happened?"

"They're going to sedate and intubate, Boomi."

"What does that mean?"

Her gaze fluttered across the room, like a bird looking for escape. Finally, her eyes rested on the screen. "They'll put his body to sleep for a while and a tube down his throat, to help him breathe."

I turned back to Dad. "How long will you be asleep?"

Dad's head rolled from side to side, his eyes on the screen. His lips moved a little, but no sound came out.

"How will you eat?"

"An intravenous solution," Mom cut in. "Through his veins."

"They can put food in your veins?"

"A sugar solution," Mom said.

"So, not hospital food," I said.

"Disgusting," Dad said. His voice was barely a whisper between loud, raking breaths. He gave me a weak smile.

We stared at each other through the laptop for a while. Then Dad's eyes closed. I panicked. "Dad?!"

He opened his eyes again. "Hospital food," he said, and sucked in a breath. "Cat food."

"What?" I turned to Mom. "What cat food?" She just stared back at me, her mind a billion miles away. That's when I got it—Dad was playing Would You Rather!

"Okay," I said. "Would you rather eat hospital food every single day for the rest of your life or a whole can of cat food every Tuesday?"

Dad smiled, but didn't answer, so I answered my own question. "Cat food," I said. "I despise everything about hospitals." His smile dropped and he gazed at me. Mom nudged me. "He needs to rest, Boomi. Okay?" She put a hand on mine. "Can you say goodbye?"

I snatched my hand away. No, I couldn't say goodbye. Everything inside me was clenched like a fist.

Onscreen, Dad had rallied a last little slip of breath. "Smell you later." I stared at him until Mom lifted the computer from my hands. That was the last time we talked.

Bebe's SUV pulled onto the street. I'd told her the truth and she called it a lie. I had to talk to Denny. He would believe me. Denny would understand. But Denny wasn't at his usual spot on the sidewalk. Hot fingers of panic crept up my throat. Where was he? Why wasn't he there when I needed him? In the kitchen, I could hear Mom banging around with pots and pans. Any minute, she'd be wiping her wet hands on her jeans, heading for my room, asking-without-asking what we'd talked about.

I knew one thing, and one thing only: I absolutely, positively did not want to talk to Mom about Bebe Jacobs or ballet or my body. And there was no way I was telling her about the boombox. I had to get out of here. I had to get back. So, I reached for the boombox and pressed play. A twangy guitar, a drumbeat, a harmonica, a spreading pool of light, and then—

TRACK 14
Karma Chameleon

Here's something I was starting to learn. You can run away
from things—you can flash through time to a totally different
decade—but when you get back, the aunt you've never met
will be waiting just where you left her, hands on hips, her
blue-shadowed gaze slicing into you like a laser beam. Jeevan
sat where I'd left him, looking from me to his sister and back
to me.

And here's another thing: You can *tell* yourself to be calm,
but sometimes your body has other ideas. I panicked again.
I hopped to my feet and headed for the window, their voices
trailing after me. From Archie: *Oh no you don't!* And from
Jeevan: *Boomi! Wait!*

But they were too late. I hoisted myself back through the
window and toppled through it, alarm bells blaring between
my ears. I hit the sidewalk and ran. I heard footsteps behind
me—they might have been Jeevan's, but I didn't turn to look.
I didn't know where I was going. All I knew was that my heart

pounded in my ears, that panic sparked off my skin, that a voice in my head was hissing at me: *Run. Run. Run.*

I ran down Alphabet Street toward the big church, the pounding of the pavement vibrating through my boots and up my legs. Jeevan and Archie were out of sight. If I could hide in there—people in movies were always hiding in churches, weren't they? I made it through an iron gate and stopped. Before me spread a small patch of gravestones, reined in by iron gates. I'd never been in a graveyard before. Like I said, we kept Dad's ashes in a box on the fireplace. I tried to keep moving, but I couldn't. The air was wet and warm, like the whole town had just gotten out of the shower.

Would you rather be stuck in a graveyard or running through a haunted house? That day, I would have chosen the haunted house. But just then, I tried to move, but I couldn't. It was like my shoes had grown spikes and clamped into the earth. It was like something was holding me down and forcing me to take a good, long look.

Here's what I know about dying:

It's permanent.

Bodies decompose. Over time, they turn back into earth. Unless they're cremated, in which case they exist as ashes in an ugly box on your mantel until someone spreads them in the ocean or over a field.

When someone dies, you have a funeral. People wear black. They get together, in person, all in the same place. Having an online memorial for Dad was just incredibly weird.

People who die live on in our hearts. That's what everyone said to me when Dad died. But guess what? That's not good enough for me. I want Dad to be living at home. In his pajamas, scrolling through news websites. In the kitchen, making me pancakes. I can't reach into my heart and pull Dad out and talk to him, can I? He's useless in there. Completely useless.

Death is alive, in its own way. It walks through the world all day, every day. I can feel it against my skin, sometimes. It has a smell and a taste. It has a sound.

Around me, the gravestones hummed like a distant choir. They smelled like too many flowers. They tasted like the residue of old milk. They leaned at odd angles. One of them had toppled over. In front of another sat a dusty green bottle. I read the headstone closest to me, its engraving nearly faded away.

Mary Hampton. Beloved wife. 1564–1620. Whose heart did Mary Hampton live in?

All at once, the earth released me. My feet sprang from the grass and I ran. I didn't know where I was going. I just needed to get away from those headstones, all those forgotten people. I ran around to the back of the church, leaped up three stone steps, and pushed through a heavy dark door. When I finally made it inside, I stopped. My chest heaved, trying to suck in the oxygen it needed. Little pinpricks of light floated behind my eyes. Was I flashing back again? No. These were just sparks of panic, pinging around my head like fireflies.

When my head cleared and my breath slowed down, I peered into the dark. All I could make out were gray walls around me, a sort of sculpture to my right. I placed a hand on the sculpture, and the cool of the white stone helped me calm down. The church smelled of smoke and rain. Through a set of wooden doors, rows of benches led up to a grand sort of wooden stage. I'd never been in a place like this.

As my eyes adjusted to the gloom, I realized I was standing on something. A flat stone slab, engraved with a name. And dates: 1664–1702. Next to that slab, another name, another set of dates. Then another, and another. That's when I realized— these were dead people. Right under my feet. I hopped to the side, shuddering.

The flat graves lined the floor, extending down the wide aisle of the main room. I clung to the sculpture at my side, and under my palm I could feel the rise and fall of the cut stone, the sharp edges and smooth valleys. All at once, my vision cleared and I could see what I'd been clinging to: a long stone bed, and on it, a man, carved of white marble, lying on his back. The folds of his robes hung down the sides of the bed. His hands lay folded on his chest. The dips and ridges of his face rested placidly under my hand. Strange to see a statue lying down. Usually, they were on their feet, in some trium- phant pose. But wait—this wasn't a statue. This was another grave. The bed wasn't a bed. It was a tomb. The man carved on top was the man lying inside.

I shrieked and shot to the other side of the room. "Nope!" I said aloud. "No, thank you!" My voice bounced against the walls as I tried to heave open the exit door. Archie didn't seem so scary now, not compared to this country club for the dead. That's when I heard footsteps clomping toward me. And a voice, from somewhere in the main room: "What's all this, then? You'll wake the dead!" A woman in a pink cardigan bustled out and gasped when she saw me. "Oh—hello, duck! You gave me a fright!" she said, bringing her hand to her throat. She was short and round, almost entirely a collection of circles, from her tidy orange curls to her spectacles to her button nose to the surprised O of her mouth. I recognized her from the bridge. She was a P&Q. But which one?

She frowned at me. "You're a bit late."

"Late? For what?"

"You look peckish."

She pulled a tin from her bag and grunted as she tried to pry the lid off. At last, she managed, and the lid flew to the floor, clattering and echoing through the church. "Fancy a bikkie?"

Biscuits. Ginger biscuits! This was the infamous Theodora Gin-Bixby of the Peace and Quiet Commission!

"No need to look so shocked," she said. "They're just ginger. Have one. Go on."

"Uh—no, thank you," I stammered.

"Oh, go on. Just one. Just one little bikkie never hurt a soul." I remembered Jeevan's warning about stale bikkies. I took one. I'd chuck it later.

"That's better. Now get that down ye, and you'd best get down there." She took a cookie from the tin and shoved it in her mouth, winking at me.

"Get down where?" I asked.

She nodded at a set of stairs behind me, one that descended farther underground. "You know where," she said. "You'll find what you need in the basement." Then she whipped around and vanished into the shadows of the church. For a few seconds, I just stood there, confused. *I* didn't know what I needed. How did she?

I looked back at the stone man. He didn't have any answers. I thought about leaving, breaking back into the humid afternoon—but where would I go? And anyway, I was curious. So I turned to the steps and made my way down into the cool, dark throat of the church.

The stairwell was pitch black. I ran my hands against the wall as I descended, to keep myself balanced, praying that my fingers wouldn't brush against anything wet or crawly or creepy or slimy. As I moved deeper underground, I started to hear sounds. First, a steady, sharp beat. Then, a single voice calling out. And finally, the rat-a-tat-tat of a hundred feet, stamping in unison.

I took one more step and halted, blinking into the dark. The steps were gone. I was on flat ground now. I couldn't see a door, but I could hear the sound of whatever it was I'd come for. So, I found a wall and walked along it, pushing, hoping for a door, guided by the voice and the sound of feet.

And that's when my feet tripped over something, and I went crashing to the ground. The voice quieted. The stamping stopped. For a few moments, the dark seemed to hold its breath, waiting. I lay on my stomach, wondering if I should get up and run. Wondering if I'd even make it through the dark.

And then a door swung open. A flood of bright light washed over me. In the doorway stood a woman in a blue sari and a green cardigan, her hair pulled into a strict little bun, her eyebrows diving into each other as she frowned down at me.

"It's you!" The words just popped out of me. But it was! It was her. Paati. Younger, sharper, angrier. I scrambled to my feet.

"Well?" she said. "What are you lying there for? Chop, chop! You're already late!" She turned back to the room, where ten pairs of eyes stared out at me. I looked around. They were kids, all around my age, all brown like me. I took my shoes off. I'd tripped on someone else's shoes. Eleven pairs of shoes, neatly lined up. I stuck my boots on the end of the row and walked out of the dark, into a vast, bright room, toward something completely different.

Could I have known what waited for me there? Could I have predicted that my first uneasy steps into that basement would change the future—not just mine, but other people's, too? I knew one thing, for sure—I knew it the second I stepped into that room. The wood floor, the neat rows of students, the straight backs, the faint trill of expectation: I had stumbled—quite literally—into a dance class. The other students stared at me as I took my place. Eight girls and two boys, all wearing loose white pants and green tunics. In exact unison, they looked down at my leggings, back up at my sweatshirt, then back down at my socked feet. "Socks off," Paati ordered. I obeyed.

Paati picked up a heavy wooden block and a wooden stick, then sat down, cross-legged, on the floor. Through a high window, a shaft of sun angled into the room and fell on her, like a spotlight. Even sitting, she seemed to tower over us. She cleared her throat and the dancers shifted positions, turned their feet out, and placed their hands behind their backs, their palms out, their elbows jutting like flags. She took a moment to look at each student. Then she craned her neck to peer at me. "You there, standing like a tourist. Please do Namaskaram."

I swallowed hard. "I don't know what that is," I said. She didn't waste a second. In one swift leap, she was back on her feet, and standing before me. "This is what we do before we start to dance. Right, dancers?" The others nodded. She moved through a series of steps, stamping and moving her arms in a wide semicircle. "With each step, we pay respect to Nataraja, our god of dance, then to our teacher, our musicians, our audience." Then she sank into a grand plié, right down to the ground, touched her fingers first to the floor, then to her eyes. "Final step," she said, "we touch the ground. We thank Boomi Devi, Mother Earth, for letting us pound her with our feet. Just follow along." Boomi Devi. I felt a tickle at the mention of my name. I'd always known I was named after the earth, but I'd never heard anyone say my name out of the blue like that.

I watched the other dancers repeat what Paati had done. I didn't know what any of this was. I didn't know that I was doing an Indian dance that had been around for two thousand years. I didn't know that, like with ballet, people spent their entire lives mastering this dance. I didn't even know what the dance was called. And if you'd told me its name, Bharatanatyam, I might have said, *Who, now?* Bharatanatyam is a long, impossible-looking word, but it's really not so hard to say. *BHA-RA-THA-NAWT-YUM.* See? Easy.

To be honest, the only thing that kept me from running out the door, at first, was Paati, picking up a wooden stick, cradling a big wooden block in her arm.

Whack! I jumped. With her thick wooden stick, she beat that block like she was mad at it. At first, I wondered if she was mad at *me.* But the other students didn't seem to notice or mind the deafening noise. In a few moments, the purpose of the wood block was obvious. She wasn't mad at anything. She was keeping time.

When you're a dancer, you learn to watch and imitate, almost seamlessly. You learn to follow a routine so quickly that you seem to be dancing along with the others, when really, you're just a millisecond behind. So that's what I did. The movements got faster, more complicated, arms flashing through the air, legs thrusting, all of it done in demi-plié.

Paati strolled around the room. *Whack! Whack! Whack!* She

beat out a rhythm and called out the beats: *Thay-yum-THA-tha Thay-yum-THA.*

I tried to remember my ballet rules. Be light. Light as air. Dance like a feather. Like your feet are made of cotton balls. Like you weigh nothing. Like you're nothing but a hollow puppet, pulled by strings above, your body barely skimming the ground.

"STOP!" The room fell silent. The other dancers stopped moving. One by one, they turned to look at me, chests heaving, catching their breath. Paati stood there with her block, just staring at me. She was out of breath, too. Her bun had flopped to the side, and a few strands of hair fell around her ears. "What exactly are you doing, my child?" she asked. *I have no idea*, I wanted to say. But that was obvious, so I stayed quiet.

She put the block down and launched into an imitation of me, her toes poking softly at the floor, her wrists limp. "What is this?" she asked. "This limpy-dimpy tiptoe nonsense? Are you ill, my child? Have you a wasting disease?" Her voice rose. "When you stomp your foot, don't you want the world to know?" With each sentence, she got louder, until her voice filled the room. "Smash the floor with your foot! Don't worry about Boomi Devi—she forgives you! Stomp on her! Bash the ground! Use your body! Make some noise, my child! Show me that you are here!"

I scanned the room, the other students. I expected them to laugh at me, but they didn't. They did look a little scared. "Well?" Paati continued. "Are you here?" I was there, all right.

I didn't want to be. She was standing too close to me. I smelled coffee on her breath. I could see a hair springing off her chin. My face was hot, and I felt a sob creep up my throat. I wanted to disappear. I wanted to flash away, sink into a pool of blinding light, and land back at home, back in my little bedroom, back to staring out a window, back to being nobody, nowhere.

Paati's face hovered just inches from mine. "Well?" she asked. "Are you here?"

"Yes."

"Yes, what?"

"Yes, I'm here."

"You are where?"

"I am here," I said, barely above a whisper.

"Again. Louder."

I upped my volume a smidge. "I am here."

"Louder."

"I am here."

"LOUDER."

"I am here!" The sob threatened to leap out of my mouth if I went any louder.

"Louder, I said! Louder! I can't hear you, child!"

"I am here!!" I *was* getting louder. I hated this. I hated Paati. She was a bully.

"LOUDER!"

"I am *here!*" I wanted to shove her away from me. I wanted to scream.

"I CAN'T HEAR YOU!"

"I AM HERE!" I barked. The sob was gone. In its place rose anger, hot and spiky. "I AM HERE! I AM HERE! I AM HERE!" I clammed up, shocked by the scream in my voice. Paati stepped back, a glint in her eye. The echo of my voice rang through the quiet room.

"Yes. You are here," Paati said calmly. "Now please *dance* like you are here."

Just then, through the window, we heard the low, loud *BONG* of the church bell. It bellowed six times, and then it stopped. Paati looked around the room, and then, quietly, she said, "Do Namaskaram."

The dancers moved through Namaskaram on light and nervous feet, then scurried like mice out the door. Something held me there. This time, it wasn't an invisible force. This time, it was me.

The empty room stretched around us like a yawn. Paati stood squarely in a shaft of light that passed through a high window. She looked out at me, a smile playing at the corners of her mouth. "Very well," she said. "Let's carry on."

Before she picked up her stick again, she paused, and looked me in the eye. "I don't know who you are or why you've come here to my secret dance class. But I know this: You are a dancer. I can see it in your face, in your back, in your spirit." I was struck silent. No one at the Academie Fontaine had ever told me that I was a dancer.

"And now," she went on, "you have a chance to learn. This is *your* dance, whether you want it or not." She paused, let this sink in. It didn't sink in, though. I had no idea what she meant by *my* dance. How was any dance *my* dance? "Do you want it?" she snapped. "Or would you rather go home?"

"Okay," I whispered. "I want it."

"What's that?" she asked sharply.

"I said, I want it!" I shouted.

"Okay, then. Let us begin," she said, "from the beginning."

We started with the most basic of the basic steps. "Let's start with the first adavu." I got into the position I'd learned in class—a demi-plié with my arms up. And just like I was supposed to, I placed one foot on the ground, then the other. "Stop!"

She crouched down beside me. "Do it again," she said. I lifted my foot and she grabbed my ankle and held it. I almost toppled over. "Stamp your foot," she ordered. My arms swung wildly but I kept my balance. I tried to put my foot down, but she held it up. I tried again to push it down, but it was like moving through drying cement. "Try your hardest," she said. I strained. I pushed. Then she let go and my foot slammed to the floor.

"That's it!" she said. "Come now, once more." I lifted my foot, and she held it in her hand, and there was something suddenly comforting about this. "Push," she ordered. I didn't. I wanted to stay like this, with her warm rough hand cupping the sole of my foot. "Stamp your foot!" I did, she let go, and my heel thundered down, sending tremors up my legs. I picked up my other foot and slammed it down. Right foot, left foot. Each time my foot hit the floor, I made it as loud as possible. I shook the earth. I thundered. I was here.

She sat back on her haunches, then looked up at me and beamed. "By Jove," she said. "I think you've got it." She studied my face from below. "Sit down," she said.

"What?"

She patted the floor beside her.

"You have a body," Paati said. "A big, strong body. I want you to use every centimeter of it. Every kilo. I want you to put all your weight, all your power, into every second of your dance. These feet of yours—they're your connection to the earth. To your home. To everything you know." Then she reached over and pulled my foot toward her. She pressed her palm to the arch of my foot, and like a baby's, my toes curled around her hand. I jolted inside. It was like a streak of electricity had passed from Paati's hand through my body. I wanted, suddenly, to tell her who I was. To tell her everything.

"Is there a problem?" she asked.

"No." Could I tell her? "No." I didn't want to hug her—not like I wanted to hug Jeevan. Seeing her like this—familiar, but strange—was a little frightening.

Paati looked at me and softened, as if she knew something had changed. "Get up, then, child. Let's continue."

And so we did. For another hour, two hours—who knew how many hours?—the dancer danced and the teacher kept teaching. It's like we both knew this was our only real chance to be together.

I moved from the first level of steps to the next, stomping and stretching, thundering across the floor, reaching for rivers, for stars. I was an angry goddess. I was a graceful deer. I was a hunter. I was lightning. I was war. I felt the burn in my arms, the fire in my legs. I was dancing. And though my body never stopped moving, on the inside I was still. I was calm. I was whole.

All the while, I tried catching glimpses of the Paati I knew, the one with folds of skin that hung over her eyes, moles and freckles sprayed across her cheeks. Now I saw that Paati had always had a dancer's back. Even when she was just sitting in her chair, brushing her hair, her back was like a straight, strong board. Pull the curtains of skin away, and you'd see the dark round eyes, the sharp jawline of this teacher. Paint her hair black, and you'd see the bun that hung loosely from the nape of the teacher's neck.

The shaft of sun no longer spotlighted Paati. It had moved in a wide arc and landed squarely on me. And just as it did, I heard a door slam above, a storm of footsteps on the stairs. Voices, shouting: "You can't tell Mum! Leave her alone!"

"We all saw her!"

"Stay back! All of you! Stay—"

The door flew open. Jeevan. Behind him stood Archie, and behind her stood the teenagers from the bridge, all peering into the dance room. "There she is," Archie hissed. "I found you, Lightning Child!"

Paati sprang to her feet. "Shoo!" she hissed. "All of you, get out! Go home! Stop making so much noise! This isn't safe—"

"Mum," Jeevan panted. "Tell Archie! Tell her she can't just stick her nose into this. Boomi's *my* friend!"

Paati fell quiet. She turned to her children. "You know this girl?" She turned to me. "Who are you, child?"

"I'm Boomi," I said. Then remembering my manners— "It's nice to meet you."

With a twinkle in her eye, she replied, "How do you do?"

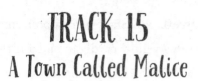

TRACK 15
A Town Called Malice

Paati wrangled all of us back up the church stairs, the teenagers squawking like seagulls, past the nervous titters of Ginger Biscuits. "Quiet, now," she trilled. "Mind your P's and Q's!"

As Paati led us out the door, the church bell bonged ten times. In the graveyard, the dark was so thick I could feel it against my skin. I held on to Jeevan's sleeve. He didn't push me away. Archie and Jeevan stayed quiet as we walked back to Alphabet Street. In fact, the whole group fell quiet. The night had doused their voices, like water over a campfire. The boys from the bridge walked in pairs, barely speaking above a whisper, if they spoke at all. Something about that was very strange to me. What happened to the rowdy scrum from the bridge, voices and bodies churning and spinning like fruit in a blender, doing what they wanted, as loudly as they pleased? Archie walked with her head down, hands stuck firmly in her pockets.

Just then, a figure rounded the corner. It stood in the

shadows and watched as we approached. I expected to find a policeman, like the ones on the bridge, with the domed hat and big black stick. As we got closer, the figure stepped into the light of a streetlamp. She wasn't a policeman. She was an old lady. She wore a yellow cardigan and a little blue hat with a flower stuck in the rim. When she saw us coming, she put a finger to her lips. She didn't say a word. Just watched us with her cold gray eyes. A chill ran down my spine.

I tugged on Jeevan's sleeve. "Is that—"

"Snodgrass," he muttered.

"Shhhh!" The group glared at me.

A minute later, we reached the steps of Jeevan's house. Jeevan, Archie, and Paati stopped, and the rest kept walking. No goodbyes, no see-you-tomorrows. I stopped walking, too. That's when Paati turned to me.

"Your family will be waiting, won't they, child?"

I lied. I had to. "Yes."

"Well, run along, then. They'll be worried. Go quietly, now."

I looked at Jeevan, who stared back at me. He knew I had nowhere to go.

"Okay," I said to him. "See you later, then."

Nobody said goodbye to me. Paati unlocked the front door. Jeevan turned to me, shrugged, and stepped into the house. At the last second, Archie stuck her head back out. "Flash away, Lightning Child! Flash away!" Jeevan yanked her back inside.

From the sidewalk, I could smell garlic and onions frying.

Paati was making dinner and my tummy rumbled. I pressed my back to the brick wall, then sank down it and sat on the pavement. I watched gnats circle a streetlamp. I had nowhere to go, no home to run to, no mom craning her neck out the window or listening for my key in the door. All I had was me. I wasn't so different from Denny, out here.

A moment later, I got up and went to Jeevan's window. Maybe he'd sneak me in, then hide me in his closet and bring me food. I rapped on his window. His light was off. No one answered. Where was he?

I'd give anything for some dinner. Even baked chicken with spinach was starting to sound good. What kind of grandmother didn't invite her grandkid in for dinner? The kind who didn't know she had a grandkid, I guess.

I stood out on Alphabet Street for a few minutes, with no idea what came next. If I knew how to flash away, I could leave. What had made me flash away before? The first time, I'd jumped. The second time, I'd fallen from Jeevan's window. Was it jumping or falling? I turned down the sidewalk, sprinted down Alphabet Street, and took a giant, running leap. Nothing. I squeezed my eyes shut, tried to relax my body, and made myself topple to the ground. Still nothing.

Then I remembered: music! Over by the bridge, music had been playing from a nearby boombox. In Jeevan's room, his own boombox had been playing. I needed to find a song playing somewhere, somehow. I set off for the town square.

From the sidewalk, a ghostly mist rose around my legs as

I walked. I felt like a house with no walls, nothing to hold me up. I could run into this night, this town, this decade, and turn into nobody. Nobody from nowhere. Back home, if I dared leave the house alone at night, Denny would be the first to stop me. If I somehow made it past Denny, Mike the ramen guy would spot me and tell me to get home. If I made it past Mike, Mrs. Ahmadi at the florist would call Mom pronto. If not Mrs. Ahmadi, then the people at Boba Dreams or the bookstore lady or the donut shop or the kebab takeout or the man who grills hot dogs on the corner. They were all Dad's friends, and now they were Mom's eyes and ears.

A chill crept up through the soles of my rain boots. I walked down the street, sifting through the mist, walking toward the old church. I made sure not to *look* at the church and its crooked old graves. I hoped to find a place—a restaurant maybe—that was playing music. The music might send me back. But when I got to the square all that met me were dark cobblestone streets, shuttered windows, metal gratings pulled down over shop doors. No restaurants. No shops open. No people. Nothing louder than the *crik-crak-crik-crak* of a sign swinging on its hinge. Thumpton-on-Soar was as silent and still as cold white marble. The night closed in around me with skeletal hands. The wind whistled into my ear, hushing me. A quiet town, for quiet people.

And then from a bank of shadows came a whisper: "Oy! Careful!" Then a stifled laugh. I peered into the dark and saw two figures hunched right up against the white brick wall of the butcher shop. The moonlight shifted and fell on two of the teenagers from the bridge. One of them was Chuzzy, who held something that looked like a tube—of toothpaste? He ran the tube over the mortar lines between each brick. He'd already done a big, blanket-sized section of it.

But why toothpaste?

From the far end of the square, I heard a faint shuffle. A lady in a blue cardigan stepped into the moonlight, elbows pumping at her sides, looking like she was on a morning power walk. In her hand, she held something small—a toothbrush. Of course! This was Beatrice Bathwater! Coming to clean the bricks!

"She's coming," I whispered, then clamped a hand over my mouth.

Chuzzy stopped with the toothpaste and turned around. "Who's there?" he asked.

"Bathwater's coming!" I said again.

Chuzzy's eyes darted from me to Bathwater and back again. Then he scrambled to his feet and took off running, his friend following at his heels.

Just then, from beyond the square, another voice: *"Boomi!"* I jumped. It was Jeevan. Bathwater stopped in her tracks, her head cocked, listening. *"Boomi! You can't be out here, Boomi!"*

I stood incredibly still. Maybe if I didn't move, Bathwater would look straight through me. But she didn't.

"You there!" she cried. "You, child! You can't be out here!" She started walking toward me, arms pumping, toothbrush in hand. And she was a lot faster than she looked.

Jeevan careened around the corner and into the square. "Boomi, let's go!"

Bathwater pulled a whistle from around her neck and blew on it. It rang like a frantic bird through the night, and the next thing I knew, a white van squealed around the far corner, charging straight for me.

Jeevan reached me, grabbed my hand, and pulled me into a sprint. The van bore down on us, gaining speed, with no sign of stopping. We sped away from the square, rounding one corner, and another and another. We slipped into a narrow alley, then turned and slipped into an even narrower alley. And then Jeevan stopped, leaned against a brick wall, catching his breath. I caught up to him, the fresh night air burning in my lungs. The high whine of panic still rang in my ears.

My breath slowed, at last. "What is *with* this town?" I asked.

Jeevan didn't answer. He just sank down the wall. "It wasn't always like this." He stared into the night sky. "It wasn't always quiet here, in Thumpton. People used to be out at night. Walking around. Making noise. Playing radios out our windows. In the summers, we'd play footy until nightfall. We'd be out past ten, sometimes, on long days like this. But then something happened. The town—the people who run things in this town—decided they didn't like all the noise. They didn't like what they were seeing."

"What were they seeing?"

Jeevan raised one hand and placed it next to mine. Side by side, our brown hands glowed in the lamplight. "This is what they saw," he said. "Brown people. New to the town, since the factory brought them in. Their kids and teenagers were all over the place. All over their lovely little town."

"So they started arresting brown people?"

"Oh, they'd never put it like that. No. They threw down all kinds of new laws. A peace ordinance. Laws against loitering, against street play, against making too much noise. Everyone had to hush up and stay home."

"And that van—"

"Would have picked us up and taken us to the police. It's happened twice to Archie."

"What happens the third time?"

Jeevan looked at me, his face dark and heavy. "Nobody knows."

"Ha!"

"What?"

"They just made that up to scare you."

"No—they didn't! There was a boy across the street who wouldn't keep quiet. He was Archie's age. I heard that on his third arrest, Bathwater and Winterbottom picked him up in that very same van, and no one ever heard from him again."

"You really believe that?"

He shrugged. "Maybe," he said. "But even if it was a lie, it keeps us quiet, don't it? It keeps us indoors, out of sight. Does it really matter if it's true?"

We sat silent and let that question sink in. For the first time since we'd stopped running, Jeevan looked at me. "I don't understand why you're here," he said. "But if I were you, I'd leave. This is no place for us."

We sat there a while longer and I looked around. A few small shops sat scattered down the alley. It stopped in a dead end.

"Where are we?" I asked.

"I have no idea," he said. "I've never been here." We'd taken turn after turn and knotted ourselves into a deep dimple of the town.

"At least the van won't find us," I said. "Right?"

He started to answer but froze.

"What is it?"

"I hear something. I hear footsteps." He got to his knees and put his ear to the ground. "They're coming closer. It could be them. . . ."

"There you are!" a voice boomed.

I swung around. "Archie!" Archie stood before us, her hands on her hips. She squinted at the window. "What're you doing outside the boiler shop?" Archie asked.

"The boiler shop? The boiler shop's on the square."

"This is the back of the boiler shop, you numpty." And sure enough, on the wall above us was a small sign that read Huston's Boiler's. I shook my head, freshly annoyed at the apostrophe.

We just stared back at her.

"Well, come on then, you little pillocks. Mum's found you missing and she's losing her nut."

"I'm glad you found us, Arch. I wouldn't have known where we were."

She sighed. "You really are as thick as you look."

Archie led us around one corner and then another and, in less than a minute, we found ourselves at the top of Alphabet Street. We'd wound around so many times that we'd wound up where we started.

As we walked up the street, I turned to Archie. "I saw your friends," I said. "The boys from the bridge. They were putting toothpaste between the bricks."

"Toothpaste?" Jeevan asked.

"Between the bricks!" Archie said. "Of course!" She let out a wild, echoing laugh. "That'll give old Bathwater something to brush with! Brilliant!"

Jeevan shook his head, but even he had to laugh. "Yeah. That actually is brilliant. I mean, totally useless, but brilliant."

Back at the house, Jeevan pushed his window open and nodded to me. "Ready for another go?"

Archie opened the front door. "You could just come in, you know. Like a normal person." Except I couldn't—Paati had thought I'd gone home for dinner. She thought I was a real kid with a real family. I joined Jeevan at his window just as he hoisted himself through it. I followed, boosting myself onto the windowsill pretty easily—I was getting the knack of it. Or so I thought. As I teetered on my waist and swung my legs into the room, I got stuck. I tried to push myself forward but couldn't budge.

"What's happened?" Jeevan asked, kneeling by his boombox now.

"I'm stuck."

"What? How?" He switched on his boombox and a tinny DJ voice gave way to a heavy drumbeat, a synthesizer, and a man's gruff voice.

I looked behind me and saw that my sweatshirt had snagged on something. "Let me just—" I worked at the fabric, wiggled it and pulled it, and all at once, it broke free. I fell backward, onto the sidewalk. My rain boots had slid off and landed in Jeevan's room.

He poked his head out the window. His boombox thumped faintly behind him. "You're not getting any better at that—" He stopped short. He was staring at the ground. "What's happening? The pavement!" The sidewalk had started to spark and glow, its mottled surface crawling with light.

"Uh-oh," I said. "It's starting."

Just then, the house door opened. Paati's voice hissed, "What's all this commotion? Where have you been, Jeevan? What—? My goodness . . ."

I got up to run away, but I was too late. Paati had seen the sidewalk glowing like a golden river. She pointed at me, and then she froze. The night grew very still, the sky filled with light. A flash. A BOOM. And I was gone.

TRACK 16
Upside Down

This time I landed on my bed—which was lucky, except that I fell so hard I bounced right off and landed on my butt, back on the floor. I looked, as always, for the me-shaped hole in the ceiling. As always, it wasn't there. I checked my arms. They were glowing.

I lay there for a little while, thinking about Jeevan and Archie, the white van and the toothpaste and the dark, quiet square. Why would Chuzzy bother with his toothpaste prank? Yes, it was kind of funny, with Bathwater and her toothbrush. But why would he risk getting caught? Why had Archie risked defacing that sign in broad daylight?

That's when something caught my eye. It was a packet of books, wrapped in plastic. On the cover of the top book was a woman on a bike, cycling along a country lane, looking delighted with just about everything: *The Real You Is Waiting!* The real me. I tore open the package and out spilled three other books, all with the same wide and friendly blueprint:

Food Journal, *Nutrition Guide*, and finally, *Weight Mates: The Program Guide*.

Weight Mates. My mom must have signed me up for a weight loss program. I flipped through the guide, past photographs of cheerful ladies, all Mom's age, doing all kinds of cheerful lady things—playing tennis, tossing a salad, stepping on a scale. Soon, I couldn't see the pictures anymore. A sour, burning feeling climbed from my stomach to my chest, like white-hot tongues of fire. I wasn't one of these women. Tears clouded my eyes and spilled down my cheeks. I didn't want to do this. I didn't want to meet the new me. I didn't want to lose weight or change my body or join some program just because Mom or Madame Fontaine decided I needed to.

My mind flashed back to my Bharatanatyam lesson, to the smack of my foot on the floor, the strong rise of my arms, the solid block of my body. Paati's words: *Use every centimeter of it, every kilo.* In that moment, I knew something about myself. The thought came to me, as clear and true as daylight. The *real me* was waiting, all right. She was waiting to be told that she was great just the way she was.

I thought nothing could get worse than that manual with its slick photographs, its columns of food and numbers. But then I turned it over. There, on the back cover, in bold italics: *You. Can. Change. Your. Life.*

Those words. Dad's words. Weight Mates had stolen them, splashed them across their stupid manual, turned them into something Dad couldn't have wanted. Without thinking,

I ripped that back page away. Then I tore the next page and the next page and the next. Page by page, I tore that book apart. I took those smiling, shrinking women with their tennis rackets and their salad bowls, screwed them into little paper balls, and flung them across the room.

From the other end of the house, I heard the front door creak open, the familiar jangle of Mom's keys sliding off the entryway table and hitting the floor. Mom. The sound pulled me to my feet and out into the hallway. I slammed my door shut and stormed down the hall and into the kitchen.

"Boomi?" Mom called, hearing my approach. My head rang. My chest blazed. In the kitchen, she was filling a tea-kettle, but she took one look at me and froze. "What's wrong?"

I'd been ready to scream at her. I'd been ready to hurl my words at her, the way I'd hurled those books across my room. But there she stood, looking reasonable and calm—happy, even. For a few moments, she stood still, just staring at me, trying to work out what was wrong.

She set the kettle on the kitchen counter. She stared at me for a few more seconds, then spoke, a nervous catch in her voice. "You saw the Weight Mates materials," she said.

"Yeah." The balloon that had blown up inside me went *pop!* And just like that, with a thin, quiet hiss, all my anger seeped out of me. I stopped being mad. I wasn't even sad. I felt my back grow a little taller, my legs a little stronger. Beneath my feet, for the first time in a long time, the ground felt solid. And when I spoke, I didn't cry or throw a tantrum or storm around the room. "I don't want to do Weight Mates," I said calmly, folding my hands on the table.

Mom frowned at the table, then used her nail to pick off a crusty speck of food. "Fine. Weight Mates was just an idea, maybe not a great one. There are plenty of other ways to lose weight. And . . . I have news!"

"What news?"

"Madame Fontaine called me today. She's decided to let you re-audition. Two days from now. You just have to nail your pointe stuff, and you're in! And we could tell them about your weight loss plans—"

"Mom," I cut in. Her words drifted away and she gazed at me. A frown passed over her face like a fast-moving cloud. "I don't want to lose weight. Not one pound. I'll give up ballet if I have to." That final sentence scared me. I didn't plan to say it. The words just marched out of me.

And were they true? They were. I wasn't just being stubborn or arguing for the sake of arguing like I sometimes do. Ballet was important, but no more important than me. No more important than feeling like myself.

I stamped my foot, just once, the way Paati had taught me. The slap of my skin on the wood floor felt good. I stamped it again, just to feel the shock vibrate up through my heel.

"You're willing to give up ballet?" Mom asked, quieter now.

"Yes."

"Well," she said glumly, "I got you these, anyway." She

picked up the shopping bag, the one that had been sitting on the counter, and placed it in front of me. I pulled out a parcel rolled up in tissue paper. When I unrolled it, the tissue revealed a pair of soft ballet shoes—not pink like the ones I owned, not black like Bebe's, but brown. A warm and gentle brown, like the fur of a fawn. "Try them on," Mom said.

"No." I set them on the table. Mom looked at her hands, hurt. I felt bad, then. I didn't want to hurt her. I just wanted her to leave me alone. "Thanks, though. For the shoes."

She nodded wordlessly, and I walked out. I'll ask the question again: Would you rather make yourself happy or your mom? That day, I changed my answer. I chose myself.

Outside my bedroom window, the sun had set. Looking down, the sidewalk was quiet. No cars on the street. The moon hovered above the park, half hidden by a cloud bank. My clock read eight. I waited for the howls that sailed over the rooftops at eight every night during the first year of Covid. No howls. Not even Denny's. The apartment was silent and still. I wondered where the world had gone.

When I turned back to the room, I saw the brown ballet shoes waiting for me. I put them on. I couldn't help it. Then I stood in front of my mirror and closed my eyes. I felt my arms lift, my legs move from first position to second to third. I moved from ballet into Bharatanatyam, stamping my feet in the rhythms Paati had taught me. Dance, the animal inside, snuffled awake. I let it move me. I let it speak to me. *You can change your life*, it whispered.

When I opened my eyes, I found a shadow lolling on my bed, sifting through the shreds of the Weight Mates book. "Gimme those," I snapped. I was about to fling them into my trash can but stopped. One shred of paper stood out to me, the sentence on it still complete: *You. Can. Change. Your. Life.* I pulled Dad's junk box from under my bed. When I opened it, something caught my eye—a folded square of white linen. I'd always thought it was an old handkerchief of Dad's, but now . . . I unfolded it. Its fabric was soft and smooth, like it had been clutched in a thousand nervous fists and wiped a hundred noses. This must have been a handkerchief from Thumpton. Maybe even a handkerchief that Paati had made. I looked for some sign of Thumpton or the factory. All I found woven in white thread were two letters. They were clear but crooked. *RG. G* for Gopalan. *R* for . . . *R* for what? I realized then that I'd only ever called Paati *Paati*. Mom called her *Maami*. Rosario called her Mrs. G. I didn't even know Paati's first name.

Why didn't I know her name? The answer was simple. To me she was the kind, quiet, helpless lady who sat where we told her to sit, who brushed her hair and didn't complain when I changed the channel. But she wasn't always like that. She was a mother. A worker. A teacher. She was *scary*. And she was sitting in the room next door. I bolted from my room to hers, not caring that she was probably asleep, that she might not want me bursting into her room. I knocked and opened her door without waiting—just like Mom. "Paati?" She sat on a chair, hairbrush in hand, looking into her full-length mirror. She'd taken her long white hair out of its braid and it spread like a cloud over her shoulders. Slowly, rhythmically, she passed the hairbrush through her waves of hair. The shadows gathered on the floor at her feet, like they were waiting for a story.

She turned around, only a little surprised to see me.

I hesitated. "Can I show you what I learned?"

I didn't expect her to answer. At first, she didn't. I wondered if she'd even understood. Then the smallest smile crept across her face. And she spoke. A real answer, right out of her mouth. "Show me."

My thumb met my index and middle fingers, my ring and pinkie fingers stretched to the ceiling. I stamped one foot and the shadows scattered like startled cats. I stamped the other foot and moved through the Namaskaram, the opening dance, that Paati had taught me. I sank into a grand plié and touched my fingertips to the ground, thanking the earth, before rising to standing again. I felt strong, solid—like all of Earth and time and space were gushing from the ground up through my heels. The body that was too big for Madame? It was just the right size for Paati. Just the right size for me. I was big. My body made noise when it hit the ground. It filled the room around me. And it wasn't going anywhere. That's just how I wanted to be, I realized. Thunderous. An angry goddess. A lightning bolt. A giant. When I stamped my foot, I wanted birds to fly from their branches.

Normally, in ballet class, I needed a mirror to look into, to know if I looked right. But I didn't look into Paati's mirror. I just closed my eyes and stamped through the routines she had taught me. I let the air and the ground guide me. I listened to the stretch of my fingers, the angles of my knees, the smack of my feet on her wood floor. Paati slapped her hairbrush into her palm, keeping time.

And then I opened my eyes. Paati was staring at me, her mouth half open. I wondered if I'd lost her, if she'd close up again. She did that sometimes, just—I don't know—went away. Finally, her eyes focused. She put her brush down. "Come," she said, beckoning me forward.

I walked over to her and she peered into my face. "Yes. You're ready. It's time to learn about your head." She pointed to her face. Her neck slid to one side, then the other. The movements were sharp and precise, and every time her neck moved, her eyes followed, snapping right when her neck moved right, left when her neck moved left. She showed me the nine different facial expressions and eight different things you can do with your eyes. Each one has a name and an emotion—fear, amazement, fury, laughter. Paati ran through every single one, quickly and precisely. I hadn't seen her this sharp since . . . that morning. Four whole decades ago.

"Your turn," she snapped, like she was back in the church basement. "Pay attention, please. No more scheming and dreaming. Left-right-left-right-sharp-sharp-GOOD! Think mischief. You have plenty of it, this I know. Let that mischief light up every movement." And so I did. I didn't know I could, but I did.

And then she sat back, smiling wider than I'd ever seen her smile. "By Jove," she said, "I think you've got it."

A knock, and the door flew open. Mom. She looked from me to Paati and back to me, trying to figure out what was happening.

"Was Paati—? I thought I heard . . ." Her voice trailed off. She stared at Paati, who smiled absently at the wall and picked up her hairbrush. Mom looked to me. I just shrugged. Mom sighed. Her eyes flitted to my ballet shoes, which I'd forgotten about completely. "You're keeping Paati awake," she said curtly. "And if I'm going to return those shoes, you'll need to take them off."

I waited for Mom to pad back down the hall. I turned to Paati, who'd gone back to brushing her hair. "Good night," I said.

She looked up at me, then cocked her head. "Archana," she said. "Come here, please."

I whipped around to face Paati. "What did you say?"

She gestured me forward. I couldn't walk away. As I drew near, she reached for my hand and pulled me in. Then she looked into my eyes. "You're a good girl, my *chellam*. I'm very proud of you." She gave my chin an affectionate pinch and smiled, then let me go. "Now get to bed, please." She turned back to her mirror. "And tell that Jeevan to switch off the telly."

Jeevan. Dad. I ran back to my room and slammed my door, the panic rising again. I crouched on the floor, my heart pinging around my chest. I ran to the window, searching for Denny. Denny would know what a load of bull honkey this was. Denny would understand. But he wasn't there. This time it wasn't panic I felt. It was anger. Denny couldn't just be there when he felt like it, and then not be there when I needed him! He couldn't just give me a time-traveling boombox and disappear! He had to know that I'd need to talk to him. He had to know he was the only person I *could* talk to.

I sighed, went to my bed, and pulled out the boombox. There was only one thing I could do. Paati had no idea what decade we were in. Her mind was skidding through time like a bike that had lost its brakes, but she had a point. Dad should have been here, *really* watching television. He should have been here with me.

You can change your life.

I *could* change my life. I could fix everything. And now, I knew just what to do. I couldn't believe I hadn't thought of it before.

I pressed play. A synthesizer, three notes climbing up, three notes climbing down again. The ground shook, the floor flooded with light. The stillness. The BOOM.

TRACK 17
Abracadabra

My landing was all cracks and scrapes this time. I fell right into the bush by Jeevan's front door. This time, those twitching curtains were flung apart. Doors were opened. The people of Alphabet Street stepped out of their doors and onto the sidewalk.

Among the dozens of people who'd moved in to gawk at me, there stood three old Indian women. One of them, in a sari and overcoat and sneakers, pointed one crooked brown finger at me. "She's a devi! She's a goddess who's come to Earth!"

"Not a devi," said the woman beside her. "A devil!"

The third joined in. "She's a djinn! See how her skin sparks with light! She's magic!"

"Not magic—a menace!"

"A rakshasi!"

"A yakshini!"

"A miracle!"

"A travesty!"

137

Whatever I was, Paati was not amused. She ignored her neighbors and rose above me, straight and solid as an old bell tower. For a few endless seconds, she just stood there, staring down at me. "And?" she said. "You're just going to sit there, are you?"

My mouth went dry. "Is that a rhetorical question?"

"Up. Now."

Without a word, Paati pulled me into the house. Jeevan sat on the entry stairs, looking like the blood had drained from his face, down his body, and dripped out through his toes. "I think we're in trouble."

Paati led us into the sitting room, with its fuzzy wallpaper and armchairs with tassels. The television stared out at me, blank-faced. On it sat the old picture of Archie and Jeevan, both of them combed and pressed and dimpled.

"Sit," Paati commanded. She sat in an armchair. Carefully, I lowered myself onto the red sofa that faced her, its plastic cover creaking under my weight. Jeevan perched beside me.

"Well?!" she snapped. I jumped.

"Well . . ." I began. I didn't know where to start. Or where to end.

"This is Boomi," Jeevan blurted.

"That," Paati said, gazing coolly at her son, "is the only thing I *do* know. Tell me, Boomi. What were you doing falling from the sky and into my hydrangea plant?"

"Well, I guess . . ."

"She's visiting!" Jeevan cut in.

Paati cocked an eyebrow. "I see. And is she visiting *us*?"

"No," I said quietly.

"What was that?"

"I'm not—" My nerves held my voice in their grip. I couldn't get the words out.

"She's joining my class, Mum, and the headmaster asked me to walk Boomi through last year's coursework, to make sure she's all caught up."

Paati turned to me. "This is true?"

No. "Yes."

"I see." She studied us for a few seconds. "Well. It's very clear you're both lying through your rotting little teeth, but I'm sure the truth will show itself soon enough." She turned to me. "Now. Boomi. I'm guessing this is short for Boomika, Mother Earth. The meaning of your name tells me that you are a practical girl, and not susceptible to the kind of foolish predicaments my son seems to encounter at every turn."

"Oh, I'm very susceptible to foolish predicaments," I said. The words had come unstuck.

"And have you a place to go this evening? Have you a home?"

I opened my mouth—usually when I open my mouth, *some* kind of answer flies out, even if it's the wrong one. But here, now, with Paati staring me down, I could neither lie nor tell the truth. I closed my mouth again.

"I see," Paati said, as if I had answered. She crossed her arms and stared at me for a long time. And I mean a *long* time.

So long that I wondered if things had frozen and I was about to flash away. Then she took a deep breath and let out a long sigh. "You'll tell me the truth when you're ready." She studied me closely. "I expect you come from a broken home," she said. "Or some sort of unfortunate situation. This could, of course, be a complicated attempt at burglary."

I scowled. I was *not* about to steal her low-tech eighties gear.

"But it's clear enough that you have no place else to go. So, you will stay here tonight. You can sleep in Archana's room." With that, she rose and left the room.

Jeevan let out a whoosh of a sigh.

What do two twelve-year-olds do on a Monday night in Thumpton-on-Soar, England, 1986? They watch telly, that's what. I ate Paati's chicken curry with buttered toast and it was the most delicious dinner I'd ever had or will ever have. Later, Jeevan brought me a bowl of Ricicles and we watched something called *Fingermouse* and *Only Fools and Horses*. Jeevan laughed so hard he had to roll into a ball, like he'd been punched in the stomach. He had exactly four channels and had never heard of streaming. Or screen time. Nor did he have a bedtime. It was almost midnight. I thought back to all the times Dad had pressed pause on *The Simpsons*, midshow, mid*sentence*, just because it was eight p.m.

I tried to watch TV and tune out the rest of the world. I tried not to think about what I had to tell him, because every time I thought of it, my stomach churned and twisted, and my ears started to ring. But the thought of that sentence, *You can change your life*, grew and grew until it filled my head from ear to ear, until I couldn't think of anything but what I had to tell Jeevan. I couldn't wait any longer. I just couldn't. So finally, during a commercial for Dime Bars, I turned to him and said, "I need to tell you something."

He looked at me. "Go on, then," he said. "The adverts are almost over."

I shifted in my seat. What would I start with?

"Okay. So, in the future, there's this thing called Co—"

And just like that, the room flashed. It BOOMed. And I was gone.

TRACK 18
The Reflex

I landed back in my room. "No!" I cried. "I have to get back!"

I pulled out the boombox and pressed play. Rumble-flash-BOOM and I was back. Back in the sitting room, back in front of the television, Jeevan staring at me like I'd just sprouted horns.

"Oh, don't look so shocked," I snapped. "You should be used to this by now." On screen, a military general with a pouty face was shouting something over the tinny roar of television laughter. "Listen to me, Jeevan—"

"Jimmy."

"Jimmy. Listen to me. When you get older, you're going to get this illness. It's called—"

FLASH. BOOM.

I whomped back onto my bedroom floor, my head spinning, my arms sparking and crackling with light. I had to keep trying. I was going back. It didn't matter that I didn't know what I was doing. It didn't matter that I might mess things up forever. All I knew was that *this* was my chance to save Dad. *This* was my chance to save myself from the shadows; the sad, quiet house; the horrible green box of ashes waiting on our fireplace mantel. This was my one and only chance to Change My Life. I pressed play.

Flash and boom and Jeevan, his eyes sparking with reflected light. The living room rug was a lake of molten lava. Jeevan was perched on the arm of the sofa, looking terrified. "Jeevan. Jimmy. Hospital! In 2020! Co—"

Flash-BOOM and I was falling. Floating. Slowly, this time. Just like the first time, I was falling through a time tunnel, little movies swirling around me. I watched them for changes. Would I see Dad alive? Dad at my dance audition? Dad walking out of the hospital? Dad walking through our doorway, home again? No. What I saw was Archie. Archie wandering through a train station, looking up at the announcement boards. Archie sitting out on a sidewalk in a cold and dark city. Archie looking very, very alone.

I crashed down on my floor, barely missing my dresser this time. On the outside, I was all light. My whole body was setting off sparks, little lightning bolts flying from my fingers. On the inside, I knew I'd failed.

Something—the boombox or the Big Burrito—*something* wanted me to keep my mouth shut. It's not that there were certain facts I shouldn't reveal. It's that there were certain facts I *couldn't* reveal, no matter how hard I tried.

I lay on my floor, feeling the sparks extinguish themselves, watching the pool of light seep to the edges of the room and disappear. I felt empty, like all my organs had been taken out. What was the point of Dad's note if I couldn't warn him? What was the point of any of this?

"Denny," I said aloud. Denny had started all this and then disappeared. He had to tell me what to do now. As if he'd heard me, a howl sailed up from the sidewalk below.

When I went to my window and saw Denny down on the sidewalk, I wasn't relieved and I wasn't happy to see him. Oh, no. I was angry as a storm. I burned like lava. I boomed inside, like thunder. Where had he been? I needed him!

I ran down our stairs and banged through the front door. "Denny!" I yelled. He jumped.

"Jeez Louise, Boomi-kid. I almost jumped outta my skin—"

"Denny, where have you been?"

He frowned. "What?"

"I went back to 1986 and took dance classes with Paati and then back in our time she was talking, like she was totally normal, but then she thought I was my aunt and she thought my dad was alive and then I flashed back again and tried to warn him about Covid so he wouldn't get sick but the stupid boombox or whatever kept pulling me back before I could tell him what I needed to tell him and I had to talk to someone, Denny, but you weren't here—"

I stopped, out of breath.

"Boomi-kid—"

"No! Don't Boomi-kid me! Who was I supposed to talk to about all this? My *mom*? You were supposed to be here and you weren't! Where were you?" The question hung in the air between us.

Denny just looked at me blankly and shrugged. "Busy, I guess."

Busy? *Busy?* Before I could stop myself, I launched myself at him.

"Hey!" he snarled. He caught my hands and held me off. "What the heck's the matter with you?" I tried to kick at him, but he swiveled away. "Stop that! Stop it!" I flung my leg out, trying for one big whack in the shins, but he shoved me away. I fell hard on the sidewalk.

"Okay," he barked. "So I was gone a few days. I'm sorry you thought I'd be here, but guess what? I'm not your magical-homeless-dude-genie just waiting on the sidewalk for you to wander down with a question! I got stuff to do! And you can't come down here and—and *attack* me when I go off to do it!" He fell silent, his rant still echoing. He looked at me, catching his breath, his face twisted with disbelief.

Sometimes, it's possible to know that you're right, but to also know that you've behaved badly. I wasn't a storm anymore. I wasn't lightning or thunder. I was a river of sad sludge. I looked at Denny's face. I'd never really looked at his face, I realized. His eyes sat in a bed of wrinkles, creases trailing all the way out to his ears. His rosy cheeks were actually a mottled mosaic of oranges and pinks and whites. His green baseball cap was frayed along the bill. He had a crumb of bread or something stuck in his beard.

"I'm sorry," I said.

"I'm sorry, too," Denny said. "Sorry I wasn't here when you needed to talk."

I nodded. Denny rummaged in his rucksack and pulled out a bag of chips. "Dorito? They're Cool Ranch."

"No, thanks."

He pulled the bag open and popped a chip into his mouth. "What're you doing down here anyway? You know you're not supposed to be out here—"

"I know, but I need to ask you something."

"Hit me."

I eyed the lit windows on our side of the house. Mom would start searching for me any second. I had to be quick. "What's the point of the boombox?"

"How d'you mean?" he asked.

"If I can't use it to save Dad, then what do I have it for?"

"You think that's what you're supposed to do? Save your dad?"

"I don't know!" I pulled the message from my pocket. "This says, *You can change your life*. But how?"

He stared at me for a few seconds. "Well, don't look at me, kid. I ain't got the answers."

His eyes shifted to the message. "Lemme see that thing."

I handed him the message. He stuck another Dorito in his

mouth, tucked the chip bag under his arm, and pried apart the folds of the note.

"Careful," I warned. "Don't tear it!"

"He folded the thing good and tight. On this thin old paper, too." Denny studied the message, squinted at it, sniffed it, blew on it. "Huh," he muttered.

"What?" I asked.

"What?"

"Denny! What do you think?"

He peered at the paper. "Your dad had good handwriting. Unusual for a doctor."

"That's it?" I snatched the note from him.

"Hey, Boomi-girl." Denny scratched behind his ear, then looked up at the moon. "I know I can seem a little, you know, *out there* sometimes. But I see you. I know you're searching for an answer, and that answer means a heck of a lot to you. I'm just not the guy who can give it to you. Does that make sense?"

"Yeah. I guess. But who's the guy?"

"*You're* the guy, Boomi. No one knows the answer better than you. And sometimes it's just a matter of cooling your jets and letting an answer come to you, you know? No point sprinting into brick walls. Let the truth reveal itself."

"Okay." I knew he was right.

"Does that help at all?"

"Not really."

"You know what could help?"

"What?"

Denny pointed up at the moon, tipped his head back, and let out a high, clear howl. He turned to me, a big silly grin on his face. "Your turn."

"No one howls for health workers anymore. That's very 2020."

"Just howling 'cuz it feels good," he said, gazing up at the moon. "Look at her up there." The moon was growing brighter and sharper than ever. A cloud passed over it, dimming its light.

I shook my head. "No, thanks."

His face fell a little. "You go on up now."

I climbed the steps. "Later, Denny."

"Anytime, Boomi-girl." As I closed our door, I heard Denny let out one more long and lonely howl.

TRACK 19
Together in Electric Dreams

That night, I lay awake and looked out my window at the half-hidden moon. Being yanked back and forth through time is exhausting—sleep pulled at every tendon in my body—but my mind still raced with questions. I heard footsteps in the hall outside, and for a second, a forgetful little bit of my brain thought that it was Dad, coming to say good night. I turned to look at the stretch of wall where he'd sit each night. In his place sat a shadow, its chin resting on its knees.

My door opened. Mom. "Knock, knock," she said softly. "Are you awake?"

I nodded.

She perched on the edge of my bed for a few long, quiet minutes. "Are you still awake?"

"Yes, Mom," I muttered into my pillow. "What do you want?"

"I saw that you—were you—were you dancing in Paati's room today?"

149

"Yeah."

"But that wasn't ballet."

"No. It was Bharatanatyam."

"That's the dance that your Paati used to teach. But how did you—"

"Mom?"

"Yes?"

"Paati talked to me. Like real sentences, like nothing at all was wrong with her."

"People with dementia do that at times, Pickle. Something from their younger days will come back to them, and they'll leap out at you like they never had dementia at all."

"And then what?"

"Well, then they go back inside themselves."

"But I'd never heard Paati talk like that. Even when she wasn't very sick—"

"I know. The not-talking, that's partly her dementia. But partly, it's just *her*."

I couldn't help but think of Paati in Thumpton, that demanding, sharp-tongued tower of a person. "I don't get it. I don't get why she's like that."

"Dad said that she stopped talking a long time ago. When he was twelve. A sentence here or there, when necessary, but it was around that time that she sort of just . . . stopped. Stopped talking. Stopped trying. That can happen, you know, when people get sad—" She stopped abruptly, like she'd caught herself saying too much.

"Why was she sad?"

Mom smiled through the dark. "The country she lived in at that time—"

"England?"

"Yes, England. It was a good place, in some ways. I'd give anything to go back to those days. But it wasn't an easy place for people like us. Not back then." She paused. "This is quite a big topic, Boomi, and it's getting late. Time to close those big brown—"

"Mom! Tell me why she got sad!"

She sighed. "It's complicated."

"It was Archie. Right? It has to be!" I felt Mom listening through the dark, like she was waiting for me to say the right thing. "She never visits us. She's like a stranger. I've never even seen her in person! Why?"

"Sometimes families drift apart. That's all."

"But what happened?"

"Well, Archana left home. . . ."

"And vanished forever?"

"No! We get Christmas cards from her, don't we?"

"Oh, yeah."

"Archie and your dad—they just weren't close. Nothing *happened*."

"They didn't fight?"

"Not really."

"So they just didn't like each other," I said.

"From what I understand, your aunt was . . . difficult. Your father wasn't. They were very different people."

"But that doesn't—"

"*Bzzzt!* Game over. Sleepy time." Mom kissed my forehead and stood up. "Night night, love."

Before she left, she turned to me one more time. "Sometimes things get so knotted up that nobody remembers where the knots started, and nobody knows how to undo them."

My door clicked shut.

The shadows gathered around my bed, all of them terribly intrigued. *I do love a good mystery,* they hissed to each other. *Whatever do you think that all meant?* They turned to me, as if I had the answer.

"I don't know. Leave me alone. Stupid shadows."

But it must mean something! You were there, weren't you? When your dad was twelve? Paati wasn't clammed up then, was she? What could she have lost?

"Go to sleep," I said to them. "You have a big day of being creepy tomorrow. You'll need your sleep." I turned over and closed my eyes.

The shadows slinked away, but their questions lingered. *What could Paati have lost? And why did Dad leave that message in the boombox? And what are you looking for, Boomi, in that crumpled old bit of paper? What's it trying to tell you?*

I sat up. Let the answer come to me, Denny had said. Paati shutting down. A crumpled bit of paper. The two things had to be connected. But how?

I thought back to the shadows' question. A crumpled old

bit of paper. It *was* old. That's just it. It was old! I jumped out of bed and pulled out the junk box. In it was the candy velocity diagram. I also pulled out Dad's note, the one from the battery compartment, and sure enough, it was on the same paper, yellowing and faded, its fibers worn soft with time. Dad's note to me wasn't written when he got Covid. The thing I was supposed to change had nothing to do with Covid. Dad wanted me to change my life because of something that happened when *he* was twelve. But what was it? What happened? Or—more likely—back in Thumpton-on-Soar in 1986, what was *about* to happen?

TRACK 20
Come Dancing

I crawled into a deep, dark cave of sleep, like I hadn't closed my eyes in days.

When I awoke the next morning, my stomach let out a roar. In the kitchen, Mom was filling her water bottle, getting ready for her morning lessons.

"Made you a fruit salad, Booms. And I found some great workout videos online. I thought you might try one today!"

"Thanks, Mom." There was no point arguing. I walked past the fruit salad and opened the freezer. There they were—my toaster waffles, somehow saved from Mom's great toss-out. I plunked four in the toaster. I turned to find Mom staring, debating whether to say something. I beat her to it. "The fruit salad will go great on top of my waffles," I chirped. "Do we have any whipped cream?"

She clamped her mouth shut and zipped her cello into its case. "Rosario will be here any minute, okay? Just keep an eye on Paati." At the door, she turned and glanced at my feet.

"Glad you're breaking those in," she said. I hadn't even realized I was still wearing my brown ballet shoes! Mom shut the door. On the back of our door hung a full-length mirror, and when the door closed, I caught sight of my feet in the shoes. The warm brown cloth cupped the curves of my feet in a way the pink shoes never had, in a way that black shoes never would. I'd never seen my feet blend into my ballet flats like this. Maybe that doesn't sound like a big deal to you, but to a ballet dancer it kind of is. When we dance, we try to make everything look as effortless as we can. We might be humans with legs and arms and joints and bones, but we try to look as unbroken as water or vapor or wind, like something that moves without thinking.

I stood in front of the mirror, arranged my feet into fifth position, then started on my warm-up. I flexed my toes and pointed them. Flex, point, flex, point.

I heard a shuffle behind me and turned. It was Paati. She'd been watching me. Her hair fell in a neat braid over her shoulder. She was wearing a pink tracksuit. Standing at the kitchen counter, she looked almost like the sort of grandma I'd see around the neighborhood, the kind who'd meet her friends every morning for a latte and a speed-walk around the park.

"Hi, Paati."

She just smiled a little and sat at the table. I scurried over to sit down next to her. I had a couple minutes before Rosario arrived. Here was my chance.

"Paati," I said. "I have to ask you something."

She just gazed back at me.

"Why'd you stop talking?"

Paati just frowned and plucked a napkin from the stack on the table. With shaky hands, she smoothed it down, then tore at its corner.

I pushed. Maybe I shouldn't have, but I didn't have time and I needed an answer. "You used to talk a lot. I know that for a fact! You used to be bossy and say things like *By Jove*." Paati's eyebrows jumped, but she focused on her napkin, tearing strips off it. "What happened?" I asked. "Did you—did something bad happen?"

Paati's eyes snapped at me. She started to shake her head, slowly at first, then faster. Faster and faster, like she was trying to shake a memory out of her brain. "No," she said, her voice shaky and low. "You mustn't." She grew still, then peered deeply into my face. "You mustn't." Tears formed in her eyes. She stared right into me, like she was looking right through me. A gale of anguish rose from her like a tidal wave. "You mustn't, I tell you!" She stood up, knocking her chair over.

I backed away. "Paati—"

"Come back here," she screeched. "You come back here!" And then she burst into tears.

"Paati, it's okay." I started to panic. "Paati, stop, it's okay—"

The door opened and Rosario stepped in and dropped her bags. "What's going on? Boomi?" She rushed over. Paati was clutching the napkin shreds, rocking back and forth. "Mrs.

G!" Rosario called. "Let's sit down, okay? I'm here, Mrs. G. I'm here—"

Paati pushed Rosario aside and her voice grew frantic. "It took her away! It took her!"

I watched Rosario wrap one arm around Paati's shoulders and use the other to still Paati's hands. I crept backward, suddenly helpless, like Pandora with her open, spewing box. Rosario glared at me. "What did you say to her, Boomi?"

"I'm sorry," I said. "Paati? Paati—I'm sorry!"

"It's okay," Rosario snapped. She turned to me, her face softening. "It's okay. Just go to your room. Give her some space."

I hurried back to my room, where I couldn't do any more damage. The shadows waited for me there. *Well, that was a bit of a mess,* they whispered.

"Shut up."

I eyed the boombox, sitting innocently by my dresser. I'd have to think carefully about what I did next. I knew there was a reason for me to go back—I had to save someone from something. But it wasn't Dad from Covid. I had another purpose in the past. A shadow sat down next to me, its chin in its hands. *What's your purpose, Boomi?*

I don't know, Shadow. I don't know.

TRACK 21
Freedom

I turned the tape over to its second side and pressed play. A happy blast of notes. A man's candy-sweet voice. "See you later, Shadows," I whispered. The light filled my room and sucked me down.

I landed right where I'd leaped—in the middle of Jeevan's living room. In the middle of Jeevan's *dark and empty* living room. The television was off. Behind me, the kitchen was just as dark and empty as the living room. What time was it? Where was everyone? I hopped to my feet to explore. In the glow of my landing, I could make out just enough to get to the front entrance, where a grandfather clock stood, like an old soldier, by the door. Ten minutes to five. I understood time zones, and I was starting to understand time travel, but I still didn't understand time zones during time travel.

I wasn't sure what to do with myself, so I wandered into the kitchen, where the moon shot through the window and lit up the drying rack full of dishes. I looked around. The kitchen counters were wiped spotlessly clean. The stovetop gleamed. The fridge hummed smugly. I thought of our kitchen in San Francisco. Sometimes, Mom went to bed without clearing up. Sometimes, she disappeared into the study to play her cello or give a lesson after dinner and then she just sort of forgot to tidy up. Sometimes, I'd step up and load the dishwasher. But often, we both went to bed without even clearing the table. We'd have breakfast around the detritus of dinner and stack our cereal bowls on top of the previous night's pots and pans. Somehow, at some point, the sink would be cleared, the floor swept, the table wiped down. Or not. Now, seeing how Paati kept her kitchen, I wondered what she thought of ours.

"Hey!" A whisper, from somewhere in the dark. "Lightning Child!" There, beckoning from the stairwell: Archie. "What time d'you call this?"

"I call it four fifty a.m."

"Where'd you go off to tonight? Jimmy said you were here and then you just . . ." She looked around. "And how'd you get back in?" I watched the answer settle into her mind. Her eyes flickered, and her mouth dropped open a little. "Hold on—did you . . . ?"

"Yeah. I flashed away." She wasn't dressed for bed yet. She looked wide awake. "What are you doing up?" I asked.

She ignored my question, grabbed my hand, and pulled me up the stairs. At the top, she opened a door to a room plastered in posters. A twin bed was pushed up against a window and rain lashed at the windowpane. "Get in my bed," she whispered. "Quickly."

"But I'm not tired—"

"Quickly!" She glanced down the hall. "I'll sleep on the sofa."

She looked at me, worried. "Just don't get up until morning, you hear me? And lie facing away from the door. If she pokes her head in, she'll think it's me." I just stared at her. A warning buzzed in my ear. *Something's happening something's happening something's happening.* Then she turned to me, her eyes wide with warning. "See you, Lightning."

Softly, she shut the door and her careful footsteps faded down the stairs. It was raining hard now. The rain had a thousand voices. It jibbered on the sidewalk, jabbered on the roof, shouted against the windowpane. But all the voices said the same thing: *There's something she's not telling you.*

Whatever Archie's plan was, it had one glitch: There was zero, *nada, no* way I was going to lie in that bed of hers and go to sleep. But I couldn't just spring up and run downstairs, either. First, I made a mental map of the house. Paati's bedroom was at the end of this hall. Jeevan's was next door. I wondered if Jeevan was awake. If I snuck into his room, he might get scared and let out a yelp that would wake Paati. I sat up and looked out the window. The moon cast a glow over the street, bouncing off the windows of the houses opposite. Everything was clearer in moonlight like this. Somehow, everything was louder.

I heard a click. I sat up. From the hundreds—thousands—of times my parents left for work or got back home, from the entries and exits of Rosario—I knew the click of a front door. Out the window, I saw Archie step onto the sidewalk. She scurried across Alphabet Street, a yellow backpack bouncing off her shoulders, a duffel bag swinging at her side. Nervously, she looked left, then right, before moving down the street. Then she turned back to the house and looked up to her bedroom window, directly at me. I stared right back at her. In her eyes, I saw the instinct of a hunted animal. "Archie," I whispered. "No! Don't go!" She bolted down Alphabet Street, around the corner, into the open mouth of the night.

"Archie!" I called out. The animal in *me* was awake now, its fur bristling, ready to chase. I called her name again, through the window, though she was gone. I didn't think about who would hear, who'd wake up.

My door flew open. "You!" I turned and found Jeevan, his hair a mess of curls, his glasses sitting crooked on his nose. "How'd you get here?"

I stared at him for a couple seconds, my mind still on Archie. *You can change your life.* The message blasted itself through my body. *Archie.* My body knew. I had to get to Archie.

"Come with me," I said, and yanked Jeevan out the door, down the stairs, and onto the street. "She's gone this way," I said.

"She's just gone out to meet her mates. She sneaks out all the time!"

I turned to him. "At five in the morning? With a giant backpack? And a duffel bag?"

He stopped in his tracks. "She had bags with her?" He gazed down the street. "She's really doing it."

"Doing what?"

He looked back at me, his eyes sharpening, like a fact had come into focus. "She's tried this before, but she never made it out the door."

And I was off, running through the warm rain, following the path I'd seen Archie take. Jeevan followed, two strides behind, his feet rousing rain puddles. "The bus station," he called. "This way, Boomi!" We wound past the old church, across the bridge, past the apostrophe catastrophe. I ran past Jeevan, straight to the market square. I stopped. There were bodies moving through the growing light, carrying tables, setting up stalls, unloading crates, preparing for the market.

As I stood there, watching them, the unspoken truth clicked together like Lego bricks. Archie was running away. *This* was what no one in my family would talk about. This was the truth that hung behind the picture on our wall, behind the girl with the dimple and braids.

"Archie!" I called.

"Shhhh!" Every person in the square turned around to hush me. No one asked if I needed help, or why I was out there, a girl alone in the dark. Archie was nowhere.

Jeevan caught up to me and pulled me through the square, across the canal bridge. We stopped when we got to an open field of concrete. Before us spread a row of white buses, each parked in its own space. The bus station. People moved through the shadows, lit by the first gasp of dawn.

"She's got to be here," Jeevan said. "But which bus is hers?"

"Maybe she's not here at all. Maybe she went to a friend's—"

"Look!" Jeevan pointed to a bus full of people. Sure enough, through a window at the back, I saw an explosion of a ponytail, dark eyes rimmed in black. "It's her!"

She must have heard us, because she turned. Just as her eyes landed on me, but before they could focus, before she could lift a hand to wave or shake her head or tell us to get lost, the bus's doors closed. Its engine roared awake. With a great inhale, the bus straightened up, lurched forward, pulled out of its bay. It turned onto the main road and slipped into the gray morning mist.

"Oh . . ." I groaned and pressed my palms into my stomach, which was twisting and turning. It knew. My body knew that something had gone very wrong.

At the last possible second, I caught sight of its destination sign. LONDON W'LOO.

Of course. *They can take their infernal kerfuffle to London.* "London," I said. "What's W'loo?"

Jeevan stared at me, wheels turning. He ran up to the station manager who was just passing by. "Sir—excuse me!"

The man frowned at Jeevan and me. "What are you two doing out at this hour—?"

"Was that the bus to London?"

He plucked something from his chest pocket. A pamphlet. "London Waterloo," he said. "Now run along home—"

"Waterloo?" I took the pamphlet from him. "Let's go!"

But Jeevan had turned and walked off, his shoulders slumped. I caught up with him and he barely looked at me.

"We need to get on the next bus. You need to listen. London Waterloo. We know where she's gone!"

I could see on his face that he'd already given up. "She's gone, Boomi," he said quietly, kicking at the ground.

"What? What do you mean, she's gone?"

"She's left. Just like she planned to." He gazed out at the water, rippling lazily along the canal. We were back on the bridge again. Above us, a sign swung on its hinges. ABSOLUTELY, POSITIVELY . . . And still scrawled over it in red marker, Archie's *Get stuffed*. He turned to face me, like he knew what I was going to say. "She's made up her mind." He picked a pebble from the side of the bridge and tossed it in the canal. It plipped on the surface and sank away, out of sight. Jeevan sank down himself, sitting against the wall of the bridge. "We have to let her go," he said.

"Rubbish."

His eyes snapped up to meet mine. "What?"

"Rubbish. That's what you say here, right? Well, I say letting her go is total . . . *bull honkey!*"

"Bull honkey?"

"Bull honkey. You can't give up on her, Jeevan. This is something I actually know about."

164

Behind his eyes, something shifted. "Do you mean—" He stopped, swallowed hard. "Is something going to happen to her?"

I crouched down and grabbed him by the shoulders, making sure he was hearing me. Really hearing me. "I traveled all the way from 2021, right? Why do you think that happened? Was it to watch Archie slip away? Was it to give up?"

"That's why you're here?" Jeevan said. "You think so?"

"All I know is, we can't let Archie run away to London. No matter what."

"No matter what," he repeated quietly. "No matter what." Then he turned to me. "Okay. Let's go."

"Let's get the next bus to London!"

"I have a better idea," Jeevan said, and sprang up, his feet rousing little splashes from the street as he ran back across the bridge. "Come on, then!"

Back on Alphabet Street, Jeevan stopped short of his own house. Instead, he stepped up to a house made of pink brick and banged on the door.

"Disco Baba!" he shouted. "Disco Baba, wake up!"

Along the street, other doors and windows started to open.

What's this palaver?

Keep it down!

Children, go home!

Jeevan banged on the door once more. It swung open. A bewildered Disco Baba stood before us, his coif of hair flying straight off his head, scratching his ear and yawning. He peered into the dim light. Then he yawned, scratched his head, and slammed the door shut.

"Disco Baba!" Jeevan banged on the door again.

It opened. "Shoo! Go home. Do you have any idea what the hour is?"

"We need your help."

He squinted at us. "Is that Jeevan? Where are my glasses? This is highly irregular behavior." He patted the chest of his pajamas, looking for his glasses.

"Disco Baba, listen. We need to get to London. To Waterloo Station."

He found the glasses, gold rims and rhinestones and all, and slipped them on. "And what does this have to do with me?"

"We have no way to get there. Archie ran away."

"Ach. That girl. Just off with her mates. She'll be back."

"She's in danger!" I blurted. This was more a feeling I had than a fact. But it worked. "Danger?" Disco Baba said. "How do you know?"

"Boomi saw her. This morning," Jeevan said. "She took her bags. She's halfway to Waterloo."

Across the street, a woman in her nightgown opened her door. "Pack it in over there, will you? I'm calling Mrs. Snodgrass!"

"Seema-ji, calm down!" Disco Baba called back. He gazed at us for a few seconds, then heaved a great sigh. "Okay," he said. "Give me two minutes." He closed the door, softly this time.

True to his word, two minutes later, Disco Baba was out the front door with his car keys and a coat slung over his pajamas. We followed him to his pink truck and clambered up through the passenger-side door, the two of us crammed into one seat. I pulled the seat belt around me and tried to loop it around Jeevan, too.

"What are you doing?" Disco Baba scowled at the seat belt. "I'm a very safe driver."

"It's the law."

He scoffed, but I clicked it in anyway. Disco Baba revved his engine and disco music thumped happily through the morning as we made our way down Alphabet Street.

TRACK 22
Waterloo

Public Safety Announcement: Never get into an ice cream truck driven by a strange man in pajamas and rhinestone sunglasses. Unless of course you've traveled through time and have convinced yourself that your teenage aunt has run off to a major metropolis and your family's future happiness hinges, somehow, on finding her.

The highways were clear at six in the morning. Disco Baba sped ahead, the baubles that hung from his roof swinging and clattering against the side of the truck.

Jeevan yawned. "Disco Baba—"

"That's not my real name, you know."

"Oh. What's your name?"

"Farukh Mitaiwala, Doctor of Philosophy."

"Oh," Jeevan said. He fell quiet, thinking. "Disco Baba?"

"Yes?"

"Do you always listen to disco?"

"And why not?"

"Don't you want to listen to something, I don't know, less old?"

"Not at all."

Jeevan didn't have an answer to that. Soon, his eyes closed. For the final hour, he slept with his head resting on my shoulder. I was nowhere near sleepy, so I stayed up as the ice cream truck wheeled down the narrow motorways of England, flashing past green fields dotted with sheep, towns stacked with old gray buildings. We slowed now and then to pass through a roundabout. Disco Baba drove with intense focus, his shoulders hunched forward, his chin jutting over the steering wheel. Soon, the motorway spat us into London. Big white tower blocks pushed up against the sky. As we turned into Waterloo Station, the morning sun dangled high in the sky, its light bouncing off rows and rows of bus windows.

"Wakey, wakey!" Disco Baba called, elbowing Jeevan in the ribs. "Oy! Sleeping Beauty! Your carriage has arrived!"

Jeevan's eyes went wide as he remembered where he was, what he was doing. He craned his neck to look at the buses, all identically white with blue-and-red lettering on the sides. "So many buses," he mumbled, stifling a yawn. "Which one is she on?"

We hopped out of Disco Baba's truck and wove through the buses, checking signs. The station was a symphony of sounds—engines, voices, the growing swell of city traffic around us. The air smelled of diesel fumes and baking bread.

"Let's check the arrivals board," Jeevan said. "Liverpool . . .

Chesterfield . . . Leicester! That's the one! Terminal 3!" Just as we reached Terminal 3, a bus slowed to a stop. It let out a great sigh, like a fed-up elephant, and opened its doors. People spilled out. Tall people, short people, skinny and fat, Black and white and brown, grumpy and happy, sleepy and awake— all kinds of people! But none of them was Archie. The bus driver was the last to step off.

"Please, sir," Jeevan shouted over the noise of other engines, "we're looking for my sister. She's come in from Thumpton-on-Soar."

The driver looked around and tapped his chin. "That's Midlands, innit? That's the regional bus—come and gone."

"What? What do you mean it's gone?"

"You missed it by a minute, I'm afraid. This bus here's from Bristol."

Panic froze my feet to the ground. We'd missed her by a minute.

"She's got to be nearby," Jeevan said, pulling me by the arm. "She can't have gone far."

He was right. How far could a teenage girl with two bags get in a busy city like this? She was probably just walking down the street, looking for a place to go.

And then, as if some magic spell had whipped her up from nowhere, there she was. Archie. She headed across the wide plaza of the bus station, her ponytail wilted down by her ear, her yellow backpack more enormous than ever. Back in Thumpton, Archie had been enormous. Too big and too loud for that little town. Here, she looked suddenly small amid the traffic whizzing by, greedy dark clouds that gathered above her. She looked in one direction, then the other, deciding where to go.

"Archie!" I yelled. Jeevan snapped to attention and yelled along with me. Hearing her name, Archie looked up at the sky. Then, slowly, she turned and spotted us. "It's us, Archie!"

She looked surprised. Then she looked relieved. Then angry. Then sorry.

And then, she started to run.

We ran after her, calling her name, down the sidewalk, past delivery trucks and people walking their dogs. Her bags bounced against her body and slowed her down. Then she came to a crosswalk, cars still zooming through it, and had to stop. We gained on her. "Archie," I called, when we were just a few buildings away from her. The light turned. She crossed. "You have to come back!" I ran at her, getting closer and closer.

She turned from us, walking as fast as she could, speeding up into a jog. Before I reached the sidewalk, the traffic lights turned again. Cars revved their engines and started to creep forward. Jeevan came up behind me at a sprint.

"I've got her," he yelled. "Archie!"

"No—Jeevan, the light!"

He pushed past me and leaped into the crosswalk, just as the cars surged forward—

A horn blasted.

"Jeevan!" I cried.

"Jeevan!" Archie cried.

The world slowed to a crawl and that single moment became many moments. Here's what I remember.

A colossal red bus.

A scream behind me.

Jeevan running, launching himself into the street.

The screech of brakes.

Archie's eyes, rimmed in black, wide and helpless and—

A flash.

BOOM.

And I was gone.

TRACK 23
Edge of Seventeen

This time, like the first time, the fall was slow. I could feel that strange pull at my chest as my body plummeted down, down, down through time. And just like the first time, I was able to open my eyes and see. Like scenes from a movie, here's what swirled around me:

A colossal red bus, stopped at an odd angle. A driver rushing down its steps.

A crowd of people gathered around.

Ambulance lights flashing through the early morning.

A girl, Archie, collapsed to her knees on the sidewalk.

And finally, the pictures gave way to darkness swirling around me: a tunnel of deepest midnight. Dark so thick it hummed. So potent I could taste it, metallic, on my tongue. I fell through that darkness for what felt like years. Its cold hands reached into me, wrapped their fingers around my heart, pulled from me every terrible thread of sadness, every cry, every wail that had fled my lips from the moment I was born.

Something terrible had happened to Jeevan. I knew it. Desperately, I tried to climb back up the time tunnel, back through the dark and the past, back to that street, that moment. But I couldn't. Instead, my fall sped up. I fell and I fell until I landed with a *whomp* on my back.

When I sat up, my bedroom continued to spin. It slowed, and then settled, but the falling sensation didn't. My insides lurched and whirled like a ship on a stormy ocean. From Mom's office drifted the deep sighs of a cello. I had changed things, I realized. I had changed things in the worst way. Because of me, Archie had tried to get away, and Jeevan had chased after her, had stepped into a crosswalk just as a bus came barreling through. Because of me, Jeevan might have—

"Mom!" The word jumped out of me. I couldn't stop it. It came again and again, in waves of sound that got louder and louder until I heard the cello music stop, Mom's footsteps in the hall. She burst through my door.

"What's wrong?" Her face was a thicket of worry and confusion. She kneeled next to me. My hands were thrashing in the air and my mouth was moving, jabbering sounds and words. I heard the name *Archie* fly from my throat. I heard the words *bus* and *killed*.

"It's all my fault, Mom! I made it happen!"

Finally, Mom reached out and grabbed my wrists. My skin sparked and crackled against her hands, but she didn't notice. Her eyes were on my face, trying to figure out what was wrong. She brought my thrashing hands down to my lap. "Boomi," she said, trying to be calm, but I could feel the shake in her hands. I could see the fear in her eyes. "You're all right," she said. "You're all right. You're all right." She repeated this phrase again and again until I stopped moving.

"Jeevan," I said. "I have to get back and save him."

Mom bit her lip. "What did you say?"

I took a deep breath. It didn't matter what she knew or didn't know, if she could help me. "I have to get back in time to save him, before the bus . . . but what if I'm too late?" What if I couldn't stop Jeevan? What if I couldn't save him from the bus? The logic pushed into me like a needle. *How* was I here? If Jeevan had been killed by that bus, *how* could I *exist*? I whipped my head around the room. "How are we still here, Mom? How am I here?"

Mom's face twisted and tangled as she tried to understand. "Boomi, you have to calm down."

I pulled the boombox out from under my bed. "I have to get back!"

Mom had had enough. "Boomi!" she shouted and grabbed the boombox. I shoved her away. She thrust herself at me, pushed me to the ground, and pinned me there, her leg on my chest. "Boomi!"

I stared up at her, the wind knocked out of me. Never in my life had my mom, my chocolate-mini of a mom, judo-thrown me to the ground and pinned me with her knee. She spoke in calm, measured tones now, each sentence cut neatly into a block of words. "You are going. To explain to me. What on earth. Is going on."

And so I did. I told her about the bus station and Archie's plans to run away. I told her about the crosswalk and Jeevan and how I'd flashed away at the worst possible second, and for no reason. There wasn't music playing—it's like the boombox or the Big Burrito or *something* had yanked me away. Her face changed as she listened, her eyes widening and sharpening, her lips chewing on words that never came out. She seemed to believe me. She seemed fascinated. She seemed terrified. Finally, I stopped talking.

"Surely," she said, and went silent. Surely what? Surely I was lying. Surely there was no way a boombox could send me hurtling four decades into the past. Surely I had completely and totally lost my mind. "Surely," she said again, "you could just press rewind."

"What?"

"Rewind."

"You mean—" I stared at my mom. Did she really just believe everything I'd told her? Or was she playing along with me? Did she think this was all just a story I'd made up?

But Mom pressed on. "That's what we do, right? When we want to go backward? We push rewind!" She reached for the boombox, but the second she touched it, it sparked. She jerked back, rubbed her right hand with her left. She stared at the boombox, then turned to me. Something had changed in her. Something was wrong.

Her eyes darted around the room. She stared at me. "Who are you?" she asked.

"What?"

She jumped to her feet and started to back away from me. For the first time, I saw fear brush across her face. "No," she barked. She put a hand up. "Stay where you are. Who are you?" She ran to the window and looked frantically out at the street. "Where *am* I?" I could see her mind working at hyper-speed, trying to figure out who the girl in brown ballet shoes was, how she'd gotten to this Victorian duplex in San Francisco. I tried to get up, but when I stood, my legs gave out. I fell flat. My whole body, from the inside out, was turning to jelly.

Mom didn't know who I was. There could only be one reason for that: Jeevan had been hit by that bus. He was gone.

And now, I was starting to not exist.

Lying on my bedroom floor, I felt my strength seep out of me like blood from a wound. I reached for the boombox. From where I sat, I could see the rewind button, the square with two little left-pointing arrows. Maybe Mom was right. She had to be right. It was the only way. I pressed down on the button with the two arrows. I couldn't get it down. I was too weak. I tried again, grunting and straining, funneling every last whisper of strength into my finger. The button clicked down. The tape whirred and spun backward. With the last little bits of me, I pressed stop. Then, play.

The fast rhythm of a guitar, the solitary woman's voice,

blowing lone and wild as the wind. Light spread across my floor, pooling around my shoulders and head like warm water. I watched it seep to the edges of the room. I watched it reach Mom, lap at her feet. Mom! Before I could tell Mom to get out, before I could think another thought, the room flashed. The room BOOMED. And I was gone.

TRACK 24
Edge of Seventeen, Rewound

Only this time, it wasn't *I*, it was *we*. Mom and I fell through the time tunnel, side by side. I watched her as she fell, her hair flying up around her ears as she looked all around her, utterly and totally bewildered. We locked eyes. She reached her hand out and I grabbed it. For a few moments, we sailed through the tunnel together, hand in hand, before the force of the fall pulled us apart.

Swirling around us were the same scenes as before, but this time, they moved backward.

A colossal red bus, stopped at an odd angle. A driver rushing backward up its steps.

A crowd of people scuttling in all directions, their bottoms leading the way.

Ambulance lights still flashing through the morning.

And a girl, Archie, pulled up from her knees to stand up straight. When she moved, I saw something I hadn't seen before: a boy lying in the road, still and quiet, his legs bent at strange angles. Jeevan.

A moment later, I landed on the cold hard concrete of a London sidewalk. When my head stopped spinning, I looked around at the strangers who'd suddenly halted in their tracks. They'd all been walking through town, going to work, minding their own beeswax, when a girl had fallen from the sky. They gaped and pointed. *What's happening? We're being invaded! Call the news!* A second later—a thud behind me—Mom.

Mom rolled to her side, rubbed her palm into her lower back, and cursed quietly. She gazed around at the low buildings and the wide, curving boulevard. I could just about see the questions cartwheeling through her mind. She looked at me. She didn't even know where to start. "We don't have time for questions," I said, and sprang to my feet.

The scene was laid out for me, just like I remembered. Archie was just stepping into the crosswalk. Farther up the wide boulevard, a bus was picking up speed. And then, all at once, faster than I thought was possible, I heard a shout behind me. "Archie!" Jeevan zoomed past me, flying for the crosswalk. The bus hurtled toward him.

"Jeevan!" I sprinted after him. Just as he stepped into the crosswalk, just as the bus driver hit his brakes, just as the big red bus skidded toward him, tires screeching, screams erupting, I leaped into the crosswalk myself, and pushed him out of the way.

I had a split second to see it: Jeevan falling backward onto the sidewalk, out of danger. I was flooded with relief. But then—

"Boomi, stop!" he cried. I looked up to see the bus hurtling at me. A wall of red. Screeching brakes. A blasting horn. It was too late.

I woke with a gasp on my bedroom floor, the bus's blasting horn echoing through the room. My throat was raw, and my nostrils burned, like I'd inhaled water. The screams of onlookers rang in my ears. My stomach twisted and stabbed, the worst pain I'd ever felt, and I rolled into a ball, waiting for it to pass. I was back in my time, in my bedroom. I didn't remember a rush of light or a boom. Did the bus hit me in that other world? Was I dead over there? Was I dead over here? I touched my cheek, still cold from the London chill.

"Mom?" I called. Nobody answered. I got up and went to Mom's room, then her office. The clock on her desk read 9:12 a.m. No sign of her. Paati and Rosario were on their morning walk, but Mom was nowhere to be found.

This could only mean one thing: Mom hadn't flashed back. She was stuck outside a bus station in London in 1986. The possibilities, the questions, the magnificent multitude of *craziness* stacked up higher and faster than a Scooby-Doo sandwich. Mom. In London. Had she seen me get hit by a bus? Did she know what year it was? She'd seen Jeevan. She could be standing there, right now, talking to the twelve-year-old version of my future dad.

"Oh, holy mountain of fudge," I muttered. I ran back to my bedroom and pulled out the boombox. That's when it hit me. I was running around, touching things, moving things. I was whole. I was alive. I existed. Jeevan was safe!

I pressed play. The springy dance of a piano and a man's voice started up, singing something about a werewolf and a Chinese menu. I ran to my window and cranked it open. In the sky, a faint white moon still hung in the morning sky. I leaned out and howled. It was a happy howl this time. Down on the sidewalk, Denny looked up at me and howled right back. As the light seeped out to the edges of the room, as it took hold and I felt the faint, faint rumble before the flash, I realized something: I had forgotten to press rewind. I'd be landing right in the spot that I'd left, right in front of that speeding red bus. But it was too late now.

The room BOOMED. I was gone.

TRACK 25
Werewolves of London

A howl echoed through the city. I heard the street before I arrived—the colossal blast of a horn, the screams around me. I crashed to the sidewalk and looked up just as a red bus barreled at me. I tried to move, but I couldn't. The seconds slowed. This was it. I was going to die. Here. Now.

And then someone tackled me, yanked me by the arms and out of the street. I tumbled to the sidewalk and the bus blew past me. A heavy elbow whacked me in the face as a body landed on top of me. The bus screeched to a halt. People gathered all around, shouting, pointing, and kneeling down. Everywhere: faces, voices, hands reaching down for me, hands recoiling. *She's glowing!* someone shouted. I looked up. A line of people moved in. *She's an alien! Call the police! No, the prime minister! The queen!*

"Back off! Leave her be!" A single shout rose above the ruckus. It came from the person who'd landed on me. The person who'd yanked me off the street just before the bus hit me. The person who still lay on top of me, crushing my chest. At last, she got up. Ponytail. Big eyes. "Archie!"

Jeevan ran up, breathless, and grabbed me by the shoulders. "You're okay, Boomi!" He peered at me, his face sharp with worry. For a moment, I saw Dad. Dad, the time I fell from the monkey bars and broke my wrist. Dad, the time I touched a hot stove and burned my finger. Dad, every time I got hurt or sad or scared, every time I needed someone to hug me.

"I'm okay," I managed to say. "And you're okay, too."

Before Jeevan could answer, we heard heavy footsteps— the bus driver, stepping off the bus and onto the street. In the cold air, his breath puffed from his nostrils. "You!" he growled, and pointed an angry red finger at me. "Why don't you mind where you're going, you gormless little twit?"

Archie stepped in, hands on hips, stationing herself between the driver and me. "You leave her alone. I've a good mind to report you to the transit authority for reckless driving," she growled.

"Archie," Jeevan mumbled. "Leave off. Come on."

Archie ignored him. "You're lucky you didn't kill her, you daft prat!"

"Would've served her right," the driver snapped, "jumping into the road like that."

Archie's voice boiled up from deep in her chest. "If you're not going to apologize," she said, her eyes narrowing like a mother tiger's, "you'd best get back on your bus before I call the police."

From the crowd, an old lady with a giant handbag walked right up to the driver and waved her cane in his face. "The girl's right. You should be ashamed of yourself!" Others called out, as well. No one felt sorry for the bus driver with the bad attitude.

A passenger leaned out of the bus doors. "Can we get on with it, please? I'm late!" The driver sneered at us, stepped onto the bus, and closed the doors. The bus rumbled away, leaving a puff of exhaust, a cloud of silence.

Jeevan cupped his hands around his mouth and yelled to the departing bus, "Sod off, you daft prat!" Nobody seemed to hear him, but he puffed out his chest and stood a little taller.

On my arms, the sparks were fizzling out.

"Boomi." I turned around. Mom. I'd completely forgotten about Mom. But here she was. And she knew who *I* was! She was back to her normal self! Mom stepped forward and kneeled down beside me, beside Jeevan. She didn't look confused anymore. Worried, yes. Scared, yes. "I'm okay," I said to her.

Jeevan crossed his arms and looked suspiciously at Mom. "Sorry—*who are you?*"

"Oh, boy," I muttered. "Maybe this shouldn't be happening. Jeevan. You can't—I can't—" What I meant to say but couldn't: *You're standing next to your future wife. And you really, really can't be.*

Mom was staring at Jeevan. She looked like she was about to scream or cry or run into traffic. Her voice came out in a gasp. "Are you—you're—"

Jeevan just blinked back at her. The air grew very still. Around us, the traffic seemed to fade into silence. All I saw were my mom and my dad, together again. Jeevan watched, his eyes widening, as Mom took his hand in hers. She studied his fingers, flipped his palm over and traced the lines running down and across, as if she knew those lines. She did know those lines.

An angry wind whipped my hair into my face, slapping me awake. My mom and dad were *here. Together. Touching.* This really couldn't happen. I mean, it really, *really couldn't happen.* My existence was about three seconds away from imploding. "That's enough!" I yelled. I yanked Mom by the hand and pulled her away from Jeevan. Jeevan studied his hand, then stared after Mom. "Don't go anywhere," I called to him. I tugged on Mom's hand until she had no choice but to follow me. I got her away from Jeevan, though she craned her neck to stare back at him.

I led her around the corner. It was the only thing I could think of doing. She muttered quietly to herself. She grew up in London, so she had to know where she was. But still, she gazed up at the brown brick buildings like they were palaces in an exotic kingdom. She pressed her nose to shop windows and muttered quietly to herself.

I barely recognized her. Normally, her face was all tensed up, like a tiger ready to pounce. Now, it sat loose and limp on its bones. Her mouth hung open a little. Her eyes flitted from the buildings to the sidewalk to the faces of people passing by. She looked like a kid being led around a supermarket. She wasn't bossing me around or interrogating me. She didn't ask me where we were or *when* we were. I had no idea what to do with her, so I kept walking, hoping that she might magically flash away. I walked her past a bookshop and a record store and a man handing out free newspapers. That's when she stopped. She took a paper from him and looked at the date.

"Fifteenth July," she said. "Nineteen eighty-six." She turned the paper over in her hands, and then she gazed up at me. "Nineteen eighty-six," she said again.

"Yeah, Mom."

"How did we—"

"The boombox."

She shook her head. "What?"

"The boombox."

She lowered the paper and looked up at the buildings again. Then she started spinning in a slow circle, her face tilted to the sun. I didn't know if she was happy or sad or just confused. I knew she wasn't mad. At least I had that.

That's when I remembered Jeevan and Archie. They'd be waiting for me. They'd be wondering where I was. "Mom—" She looked over at me like she'd forgotten I was there. "I have to get back to the others. You can't come."

Her eyes focused on me, like she'd woken up from a dream. "Boomi," she said, her voice regaining its usual sharpness. "Are you okay? I don't— What are you doing here? How do I know you'll be okay?"

"I'm fine. I'm safe here." *I'm with Dad*, I wanted to say.

Then, as if she'd read my mind: "The boy. That boy."

"Yeah."

"It was him."

I nodded. "But you can't talk to him. Not again."

"I know," she said. Tears sprang to her eyes. "I know," she said again. Every now and then, Mom and I understand each other.

She cocked her head to the side, studying me. "You understand all this better than I do. You'll be okay, then?"

"Yeah."

"And you'll come back home?"

"I promise. We'll both flash back when it's time. It always happens."

She nodded slowly. "We're in London," she said. "London, 1986. Is that right?"

"That's right." Behind her eyes, something started to grow, to swell and shine like a big red balloon. Then, all at once, she broke into a smile. It was like sunshine pouring out of her. "I don't know what on God's green earth is happening right now, Boomi, but I am in London and it's 1986! I haven't been in London in 1986 since . . . 1986!" She threw her head back and laughed.

"Mom, I don't think—"

"I have a lot to do, Boomi. A lot to do!" She raised her fists in the air and let out a whoop. The newspaper man stared at her.

"Mom, wait! When you want to go back, you'll have to listen to a boombox."

"A boombox?" She shrugged. "Easy enough."

"Are you sure you'll be okay?"

But she was off, trotting down the street, her arms spread like wings, her face pointed at the sky. She spun in the air and landed, then turned a corner and was gone. I had no idea what would come next for Mom, how she'd get back or when. I had no idea if the time tunnel had caused her to lose her mind. I just knew she was happy, and at that moment, nothing else mattered.

TRACK 26
Electric Avenue

When I rounded the corner by the bus station, I froze. There stood the pink ice cream truck, parked against the curb, its baubles and tinsel spangling in the morning sun. Around the truck, a crowd swarmed—television news cameras, reporters, cameras with blinding flashbulbs. Disco Baba, not one to miss a business opportunity, was handing out ice cream bars and collecting money. As he leaned over to give someone their change, he caught sight of me.

"You there!" he called. "Hurry! *Chalo!*" He waved me over and as he did, the reporters and onlookers caught sight of me, too. They moved at me like a swarm of bees, a flurry of shouts and flashing cameras. *It's her! The Witch of Waterloo Station! Over here! Hey, girl!* I ran for the truck. I didn't know what else to do. The crowd was gaining on me, and just as I got to the back of the truck, the doors flew open and Archie pulled me up by the arms. Jeevan slammed the doors shut, Disco Baba hopped into his seat, and the truck's engine roared to life. A wall of noise surrounded us as we moved off, people knocking at the truck doors, pressing their palms to the back window. I'd seen a video of the Beatles once, and it looked a lot like this.

We were no Beatles, but we were pretty ready for some peace and quiet. Disco Baba turned up the disco as the truck wound around a roundabout. I thought about Mom. Would she be okay? She knew London. She grew up there. But what would she be doing? Was she going to try to find herself? *I'm in London and it's 1986!* I decided Mom just wanted a day without worries. I bet it had been a while since she'd had any fun.

Soon, we sidled onto the highway and the road purred beneath us. Jeevan sat next to me in the cold well of the truck bed. Archie sat across from us, looking out the high window. I wondered what she was thinking just then. Was she glad we'd stopped her? Glad to be heading home? The truck started to rock me to sleep.

"Hey, Disco Baba!" Jeevan called.

"Yes, *beta*."

"Are we really going to listen to disco all the way home?"

"What do you suggest, my boy?"

"Could you put on the radio?"

Disco Baba must have been in a generous mood. He switched the station, then cranked up the radio to a drumbeat, a man's shout, and the sound of a motorcycle revving.

Archie woke from her thoughts, pumped her fists in the

air, and let out a whoop. "Electric Avenue!" she cried and started to sing along. Halfway through the song, I realized: I hadn't flashed away. And on the drive down to London, there'd been music playing, and I hadn't flashed away then. And what about the yanking back and forth when I tried to tell Jeevan about Covid? And the flash away from the bus? No music then, either. Something had changed. The Big Burrito had officially stolen the steering wheel.

Jeevan turned to me. "You must be knackered."

I shrugged. "It's hard work being a media sensation."

"And zooming through time," Archie said.

"And nearly being struck by a double-decker in a zebra crossing," Jeevan added.

I yawned. "I didn't see any zebras."

Archie looked down at me and burst out laughing. Jeevan joined in. "Who's going to tell her about sleeping policemen?" I had no idea what was so funny, but I was too tired to think about it anymore. Zebra crossings. Sleeping policemen. Before anyone could explain any of it, I'd drifted off to sleep.

I woke with a shiver and a jerk. The truck had slowed to a stop, stuck in traffic. Disco Baba had switched off the radio and put in a tape of old Indian music, scratchy and warbly film songs that Paati used to play. Across from me, Archie was biting into the edge of an ice cream bar. It was freezing back here, which made sense. It was an ice cream truck.

As I started to wake, the question came back to me. When would I flash back? And how? And why was I still in 1986? As far as I could tell, I'd saved Jeevan from the bus and I'd kept Archie from running away. What else was there to do?

Archie threw the ice cream stick across the truck and rested her head against the wall, where it bounced and bobbed with every bump in the road. She closed her eyes and heaved a deep, rattling sigh.

"What's wrong?" I asked.

She glanced over at me. "I'm going back there, int'it? Back to Thumpton-on-Soar. It's doing my head in, Boomi."

"But it's your home," I said.

"It's a graveyard. A lovely, perfect graveyard of a town. And I'm a ghost in it. No one sees me. No one hears me. And when I'm not a ghost, I'm in trouble."

"No one wants to see any of us," Jeevan said, his head dipped deep into the freezer box. He straightened up, holding an ice cream bar.

"What do you mean?"

"They want us to stay tucked into our houses," Jeevan said. "Quiet as you like, coming and going to school and the factory, but that's it. We're all ghosts in Thumpton. Us Asians. And the P's and Q's, their people—they get to walk around at all hours, they get to fill up the town with their market and their little shops. They're the ones who get to *live*."

That's when something, a little block of logic, clicked into place. I thought back to the sign on the bridge, the toothpaste prank. Archie and her friends didn't do those things to be funny or bad or even rebellious. They did them to be seen.

I looked to Archie. "And that's why you ran away."

"Yeah. And that's why—no offense—I'll likely run away again."

"What?" A little woodpecker of panic started rat-tat-tatting in my chest. "No. Archie, you can't run away. Something could happen to you!"

"Well, chuffin' heck, Boomi, I *hope* something happens to me! I'm losing my head waiting for something to happen to me!"

"Like what?" I said.

"Like—like anything! Like noise! Like music! Like people running up to you and shouting things in your face! Like crowds and fireworks and dancing in the streets! I'm bored out of my *socks* here in Thumpton! I'm going *mental*!"

"But you're almost seventeen, right? You can leave in a year and go to college."

"A whole year! A whole year? That might work for Billy No-Mates here, mummy's angel, doing his exams and keeping his mouth shut, but it won't work for me, will it?"

"I resent that description," Jeevan said.

"It's true," she snapped. "You being a perfect mummy's boy hasn't made it any easier for me, has it?"

"Hey!" Jeevan sat up straighter. "I don't like it here any more than you do! But I don't go shouting from bridges and running off to London. I don't spend every minute of my life trying to drive Mum completely raving mad, do I? There are other ways to get out, you know!"

"Exactly! And I'm doing it my way!"

"Fine!"

"Fine!"

Jeevan crossed his arms and glared at Archie. Archie glared back. Their voices echoed between the truck walls.

So this is how it started, I thought. Archie ran away. Dad gave up on her. Paati gave up on everything. The years passed and this family of three people, who'd once been packed so tightly into a little brick house, lost its shape. Its members dripped away from each other like streams of milk from a toppled glass.

I knew why I hadn't flashed back yet. I had to fix this for Archie. I had to change her life.

TRACK 27
Born to Run

Archie fell asleep. The morning sun shone brightly through the truck's high windows.

"We have to stop her, Jeevan."

"What'll you have me do? Lock her in a cage?"

"I don't know."

"Well, let us know when you think of something." He gazed up at the window.

Ghosts. Thumpton was full of ghosts. And sitting across from me, Jeevan was a ghost, too. Hollow. Spineless. A sudden, hot spout of anger leaped up inside me. He saw the look on my face.

"What now?" he asked.

"You're a coward. You don't deserve a sister."

He scowled. "What?"

"You know she's going to run away again, and what are you doing about it? Nothing. You're just sitting there. You've already given up."

"That's easy for you to say, int'it? You just drop in here, from—from *nowhere* and you think you're going to make it all better, do you? You don't have to live with her! I'll be glad when she's gone!"

"No, you won't," I said. "I would've done anything if I could have—" My voice caught in my throat and kept me from finishing. *If I could have kept you from leaving.*

We both went quiet. Then Jeevan spoke. "What's going to happen is going to happen. So you might as well shush up about it." He wrapped his arms around his knees and buried his face between them.

Before long, I could see the big brick factory of Thumpton. We pulled off the motorway and onto the street. When Disco Baba slowed to a stop at a streetlight, Archie yawned awake. The ride got bumpier, as the truck rumbled over the cobblestones of Thumpton-on-Soar.

Guilt started its slow crawl around my heart. I'd called Jeevan a coward. Dad was anything but a coward. Now, Jeevan focused on his feet, tying the laces of his two shoes together, before untying them again. I wasn't going to change him. I wasn't going to change Archie, either. But I had to change something. What would it be?

We pulled into Jeevan's neighborhood, heading for the high steeple of the old church. I knew that as we passed down the road, curtains would tremble, faces would poke through them to see what was happening, and then they'd disappear, back to their quiet homes, their dark houses.

Something clicked on in my brain. Like the two heads of a cassette tape, a thought started to move, very slowly, very quietly. I could almost hear it.

A street full of ghosts. That was the problem. I had to turn those ghosts into real people. The thing was, I knew nothing about ghosts. So I thought of my shadows, crouching in corners, gathering around my bed at night. The shadows weren't exactly ghosts, but they were the closest thing I knew. What did the shadows like? They liked me. They liked people moving around, living. What did *living* mean, though? In my head, the cassette tape hushed with static, just waiting for a song to break through. I remembered the day I flashed away from Alphabet Street, the crowd that had run out of their houses, drawn to the sidewalk by the spectacle. People were chattering, calling out, making *noise*. No one minded their P's and Q's then. And the crowd outside the bus station, the flashing cameras, the palms against our window, the bodies pressing into the ice cream truck. All those people *wanted* something. They *moved*. They made *noise*.

"Noise," I said aloud, chewing the word over, letting it stick in my teeth like a caramel. And then, all at once, there it was: "Noise!"

Archie turned to me. "What're you on about?"

"You don't want to know," Jeevan muttered, though his eyes rested on me, waiting.

"Listen, you two." I crouched down next to them. "I've

learned something in all this flashing through time. You know what it is?"

Jeevan raised an eyebrow, waiting.

"If you want something to change, you've got to change it," I said. "There's no point running away from the things you don't like. We need to do something. Something more than toothpaste. Something more than vandalizing signs." I looked from Archie to Jeevan. "I have an idea. Will you trust me?"

Archie thought for a moment, then traded a glance with Jeevan. She shifted uncomfortably. "Okay, Lightning Child. Show us what you've got."

"Disco Baba!" I shouted.

Disco Baba jumped and hit the brakes. "You'll give me a heart attack, child."

"Stop here!" We were just outside the church.

"But this isn't your home."

"That's okay. We need to stop. And you'll need to put on your outside music speakers. And you'll need to put on the radio."

"Oh, I will, will I?" he asked haughtily. "I have a reputation in this town, my child. They call me Disco Baba. Not 1986 Baba."

"Please, Disco Baba." I made my eyes all big and sad, like a kitten stuck in a well. "For Archie."

He shook his head, muttering to himself, but reached out and stopped the Bollywood. Then he twiddled the radio dial until the right station crackled to life. The racing beat of a snare drum, a guitar, and a melody that sounded like a tropical holiday.

"Boomi," Jeevan said. "What're you on about?"

I opened the truck doors and the day blasted in, sunny and brisk. Behind us spread the quiet graveyard, the church steeple that pierced the sky. I looked back at Jeevan. "We're going to change things."

Something in his face shifted, like he was starting to understand. "Do you have a plan?" he asked.

"Yes." This was only a half-lie.

"Will it work?"

"I don't know." This was the total truth. In that moment, all I really knew was that the music trailing from the radio was way too quiet. "Turn up the volume, Disco Baba."

"No, thank you, strange girl," he called back. I turned to Jeevan. We just looked at each other for a few seconds. For the first time, I felt like he got me. I felt like he was my friend.

Jeevan sprang to his feet and hopped out of the truck. He walked up to the driver's-side window. "Go on, Disco Baba! Crank up the tunes!"

Disco Baba turned around and cast a grumpy eye over Jeevan, who stood with his glasses askew, one lens fogged up, peering hopefully up at the truck. Disco Baba couldn't help it. He smiled. Then he reached out and turned the volume up higher, higher, as high as it would go.

Jeevan turned to me. "That better?"

"Definitely. Follow me!" I ran up Alphabet Street, knocking

on every door. Jeevan didn't ask why. He didn't argue. He just ran past me and knocked on more doors. Archie stood at a distance, watching. Then she sprang into action, too. She crossed the street and banged on every door she could.

Music flew from the truck down Alphabet Street and, sure enough, one by one, doors began to open. People stepped onto the sidewalk, looking around, confused. They saw their neighbors. Something was happening. They could have all shut their doors and gone back to their own beeswax, but they didn't. Instead, one by one, the people of Alphabet Street shuffled out of their house slippers and into their shoes, and went to witness the infernal kerfuffle. They walked up Alphabet Street, toward the truck. It was both a strange and familiar sight for them. They saw Disco Baba's Ice Cream Wonders, which had rattled down this road every day of every season for as long as they could remember. But this time, children were calling them to come out. This time, the usual disco was replaced by a thumping snare drum that laughed from his speakers, a happy melody that climbed to the clouds.

These were the faces behind the curtains, the shadows behind the doors. There must have been a hundred people out, old and young, wrinkly and smooth, smiling and scandalized and amused and bewildered.

They gathered in a crowd in front of the ice cream truck. But here's the thing: They just stood there, like they were waiting for a bus. Archie walked up behind me. "This is your big idea?" she asked. "Play some loud music? Get the P's and

Q's out here to arrest Disco Baba?"

My stomach sank a little. No. This wasn't my big plan. My big plan wasn't quite working. I don't know what I expected, but it wasn't this. It wasn't just a bunch of brown people standing around, looking at us, looking at each other, while pop music played loudly for no apparent reason at all.

That's when Paati walked out of her house, striding down the street, straight backed.

Paati!

Paati turned to me. "I don't know what you're playing at, child, but this music isn't *our* music."

She was right. Sometimes, an answer just walks right up to you. Here's what I realized: Back in San Francisco, Paati had woken up for a while when I danced for her, right? She'd become her old self again when she saw Bharatanatyam, when the slap of my feet on a wooden floor brought her back to the rhythms that pulsed in her like a heartbeat.

"Disco Baba," I called. "Put on that tape you had. The Bollywood film songs!"

He winked at me. "Righty-ho, strange girl. That I can do." The radio turned off and Bollywood switched on, with its hiss-thump beat and a woman's voice echoing against the brisk bounce of violins.

"Oh. Brilliant," Archie said. I ignored her.

"I have a good feeling about this," I said to Jeevan.

He nodded. "So do I."

We stood looking out at the people of Alphabet Street.

They stood looking at us, waiting for something to happen. Here's something else I was learning that summer: A big change can start with the smallest action of the very smallest person.

"Look!" Jeevan whispered. At the edge of the crowd stood an old lady with a shopping trolley, her hair pulled into a tiny bun. She wore a bright blue salwar kameez and sneakers. She had an enormous red bindi painted on her forehead. She was the tiniest old lady in the world, and she was making the tiniest movement in the world: the flick of her wrist, back and forth, in time with the music. I focused on that wrist. I prayed to the Big Burrito for that wrist to send its pulse waves to her arm, to her shoulders, to her hips, to pass like an electric current to the arms and hips and shoulders of the lady next to her and the lady next to *her.*

I knew, all at once, what had to happen. It wasn't just noise that Thumpton needed. It was *dance.*

The old lady met my eye. I raised my hand and spread my fingers as Paati had taught me. Alapadma—the lotus. The lady spotted this and smiled. She copied me, lifting first her right hand then her left, spreading her fingers. And just like that, the music caught her. She thrust her shoulders left-right-left-right, to the thrumming beat. She stepped apart from the crowd and kicked out her feet. She spun in a circle and stepped as lightly as a deer across the cobblestones. And the crowd watched. They watched in silent awe.

That's when I caught Paati's eye. I pleaded silently, *Please.*

You know what to do. As if she'd heard me, Paati moved out of the crowd, toward the old lady. She placed her hands on her hips and stepped proudly, artfully, to the center of the circle. And then she let out a laugh. She rolled her wrists, jutted her hip out, and moved across the circle, stamping and spinning and circling her arms in big, wide arcs.

The door to Mr. Winterbottom's shop opened. He stepped out onto the sidewalk.

"Oh, pants," Jeevan said. "He's going to make us stop."

Jeevan was right. What now?

Just then, a cry rose from the crowd and a man with a beard and a turban leaped into the circle, landing with his feet wide, his hands held high, his shoulders pulsing to the beat. He whirled around Paati and the old lady. He jumped on one foot, the other foot high in the air, and let out a joyous yelp.

Suddenly, a house door opened, and another man came out. Around his shoulders hung an oblong drum. In his hands, he carried two drumsticks, one straight and one bent. "Hai!" he shouted, and started beating the drum, the sound of it cracking strong and clear over the streets of Thumpton, rousing birds from their nests, rousing neighbors from their stupors. The crowd started to clap along, and one by one, more people stepped into the center of the circle. And just like that, it was happening. People were dancing. Boogying. Shimmying. Laughing. Even Disco Baba hopped from his truck and joined the throng, the sun glinting off his rhinestone sunglasses. Mr. Winterbottom didn't stop us. No one could stop us.

I turned to Archie. She didn't have a snide comment for me. She wasn't even looking at me but staring at the scramble of dancers that now spun and whooped through Alphabet Street. Everyone had joined in, dozens of brown bodies jumping and shaking and throwing their heads back like some bigger, stronger spirit had overtaken them.

TRACK 28
Bright Side of the Road

We had been spotted. By the church, a throng of people stood watching us. They didn't look like they were from Thumpton. They had wandered over from the market on the square. The thumping and hollering from Alphabet Street had lured them away from their linens and lace. Little by little, heads turned, feet slowed, arms dropped, and laughter faded. The dancing trickled off and grew still. A hundred brown people stood, breathless, staring back at their audience, wondering what would happen next.

A voice from the church gate: "We should have known this would happen." I turned and saw them, the Peace and Quiet Commission. Beatrice Bathwater, Sybil Snodgrass, and Mr. Winterbottom. Only Mrs. Gin-Bixby was missing. Beatrice Bathwater pulled a tissue from her sweater sleeve and dabbed primly at her forehead.

Mr. Winterbottom stepped forward and pointed a long, bony finger at the dancers. "Who's the responsible party here?"

"I am," Jeevan called.

"Jeevan—what're you doing?" I hissed. I turned to Winterbottom, a little storm brewing in my belly. "It was me."

His cold gray eyes rested on me. I shivered. "And are you aware—" He puffed out his chest and angled toward the crowd of marketgoers, making sure they could hear him. "And are you aware that this level of noise is a civil offense in the municipality of Thumpton-on-Soar?"

My voice came out in a squeak. "Yes."

He dug in his pocket, brought out a notebook, and opened it. His voice rose, trumpeting with great importance. "I shall now proceed with a citizen's arrest on the grounds of breaching the peace," he said. "I hereby charge you—" He paused. "What's your name?" he whispered.

"Boomi Gopalan."

"I hereby charge you, Boomi O'Fallon"—I cringed at the name-butchering—"with breaching the peace of the historic municipality of Thumpton-on-Soar." He took a long, sanctimonious look around. "A quiet town," he said. "For quiet people."

"Oh, naff off with your quiet town!" Archie yelled from behind me. "Naff off with your commission and your market and your lovely little buildings!"

Winterbottom breathed heavily through his nostrils but said nothing. Jeevan stepped forward. "And naff off—" His voice caught in his throat. He took a quick breath. "And naff off with your history, too—"

"What's that?" Winterbottom barked.

"I said, um . . . I said naff off with your history, too." He stared nervously at the ground. I nudged Jeevan. He looked up at me. I nodded at him. He looked around at the crowd, watching, waiting. I can only imagine how scared he was. I can only imagine what pushed him to keep going. "You know what's in your history?" Jeevan asked. "In your British history? *Us*." The people of Alphabet Street perked up, paying sharp attention to his every word. He stood a little taller. "We're part of your history." His voice grew louder. "We're here because of you. And *you're* here because of *us*."

My heart hammered in my throat. "He's right," I managed to say. "Maybe to you, history looks like a—like a postcard. Maybe you think it's something that never changes. But guess what? History is full of hidden corners. *Believe* me, I know. The past is a lot weirder than you think it is."

The other P's and Q's stood still as stone, clutching their handbags. "We're real people, you know," Jeevan said, calmer now. "We're not just here to work in your factory. This is our home, Mr. Winterbottom. I know you don't like the noise we make, or Disco Baba's truck and the music it plays. I don't like disco, either. But he lives here. And so do I and so does my sister and all these people. We're real people who live here. And go to school. And buy sweets and newspapers in your shop. So, what about us?"

And then, from inside the church gate, "Yes, Reginald, what about them?" The entire crowd turned to that voice. It was Mrs. Gin-Bixby. Ginger Biscuits. "The boy's right, you know." Ginger Biscuits opened the church gate and stepped through it. I don't know how long she'd been there, listening. "Must they keep silent forever? Scurry about like church mice? That's no kind of life for them, is it? That's no kind of life for any of us." She cleared her throat and rubbed nervously at her hands. "I hereby resign from the Peace and Quiet Commission. You may punish me as you see fit."

"Don't punish her," Archie piped up. "She's the only one of you lot who gives a toss about us. You can't pretend we don't exist. And I'm tired of hiding away. I was so tired of it I *ran* away. We don't fit into your postcard, do we? With our brown faces? Our loud drums and our clangy music? Well, maybe Thumpton's changing. Maybe it's not a quiet place. Maybe it never has been! Maybe it's a *loud* place. For *loud people!*"

An old lady with the shopping trolley let out a throaty yell that hung over us like the cry of a hunting bird. The man with the drum sent three beats cracking through the sky. He started to beat out a rhythm, and, miraculously, the others joined in, clapping along, hands raised above their heads. Disco Baba cranked up his music, and we picked up right where we left off. We danced.

No one punished Mrs. Gin-Bixby. Winterbottom didn't make his citizen's arrest. Instead, he stood with his arms crossed stubbornly over his chest. Gin-Bixby, Bathwater, and Snodgrass stood next to him in a neat line, looking very much like a postcard. Soon, the marketgoers stopped watching.

Instead, they trickled into the crowd of dancers, threw their arms up, smiled to the sky, and danced along with us. Mrs. Gin-Bixby grinned when she saw this. She said something to Mr. Winterbottom, laughed, and bopped his hip with hers. Then she let out a *whoop!* and moved in to join the dancing herself.

Eventually, Snodgrass and Bathwater checked their watches, straightened their hats, and walked off. Mr. Winterbottom dusted off the sidewalk, took a seat on the curb, and watched. Whatever fight had been brewing inside him was carried off that afternoon by the drums and the music and the warm, happy mist of people dancing. He never did join in, but I was sure I saw his toe begin to tap, and his head bop in time with the drums. He couldn't stop himself, as surely as he couldn't stop us.

Bollywood music became bhangra and bhangra became disco, until Jeevan snuck into the truck and cranked up the radio. Prince, the Pointer Sisters, Madness, and Billy Idol. Driving drums and grinding guitars hopped on the currents of that summer afternoon. They blew down Alphabet Street and right into town.

From all over Thumpton, people trailed over to our street, pulled by the noise that had, for many years, lived quietly inside them. And the people of Alphabet Street danced. Not just because they wanted to. This time, they danced because they needed to. They filled that street from door to door, they pounded their feet against its precious cobblestones. They danced to leave their mark on this town, to press into it like a new song on a mix tape. *We are here*, their dancing said. I stamped the ground when I thought of it. I laughed out loud. *We are here.*

TRACK 29
Should I Stay or Should I Go

Later that afternoon, Jeevan, Archie, and I sat against the brick wall of their house, Denny-style. Along Alphabet Street, people lingered in their doorways or stood chatting on the sidewalk, not willing to fold themselves back into their houses, back into their quiet lives. They wanted to linger with the echoes of music. They wanted to cling to that strange and wonderful day for as long as the sun would let them.

I turned to find Jeevan squinting at me. I could practically hear his brain whirring and plinking. "Not trying to be rude," he said, "but are you, like, ever leaving? When do you have to go back?"

"I don't know."

"I mean—" He picked nervously at some fluff on his sweater. "You could stay, you know, if you wanted. You could sleep in Archie's room. She's off to uni next year, anyway."

I didn't know what to say.

He looked up at me, a sheen of hope in his eyes. "Do you think you could do that? Do you think you might stay?"

Would you rather dance in the background of someone else's life, or stand in the spotlight of your own? Living in 1986, going to school with Jeevan, sharing a room with Archie, never having to return to Mom's measuring tape or Madame Fontaine or the shadows that waited with their whispered questions— I'd have given anything to do that.

"I'll get pulled back when it's time to go," I said.

"Who do you think decides?"

"The boombox. The universe. The Big Burrito."

"The Big Burrito." He tossed a pebble into the middle of the street. "What's a burrito?"

Archie stretched, leaned back, and closed her eyes to a passing sunbeam. "Hey, you know what I'm thinking? You know how, in *Doctor Who*, the doctor always has a mission?" Her eyes popped open. "Maybe that's what you've got. A mission. Maybe once you finish it, you'll flash away."

"A mission," I said. "I thought of that. But I thought I'd finished my mission."

Archie gazed down Alphabet Street, thinking about this. "Was I your mission?" she asked. "Bringing me back from London. Was that it?"

"I sort of thought it was, but I'm still here. I'm not exactly dying to go back, though. My house is boring. I have dance auditions this week and I know I'm going to blow them."

Jeevan nodded at my brown ballet shoes, still wrapped around my feet, scuffed and tearing at the toe. "That explains the shoes."

"What's so terrible about dance auditions?" Archie asked.

I pointed to my toes. "Those things."

"Your feet?"

"My feet, my toes, my ankles, my legs, my whole body. I can dance in shoes like these, but when I go on pointe, everything goes haywire and I fall."

"On pointe," Archie said. "Your tippy-toes, you mean? That's dead easy! I can go right up to the tippy tips of my tippy-toes!"

I rolled my eyes. "Well. Congratulations."

"Come with me." Archie bounded over to the kitchen window, its ledge as high as her shoulders. "How else do you think I sneak back into the house at night?" She cleared her throat, held her arms out, and slowly, inch by inch, her heels lifted off the ground, followed by her arches and the balls of her feet. She shifted forward and moved to her toes, rising and rising, until she stood, impossibly, on the very tippiest tips of her sneakers. She raised one arm into fifth position and then the other. She probably hadn't done a plié in her life, but there she was, her elevé as strong as any ballerina's.

Then, in one swift movement, she sprang off her toes and hoisted herself onto the window ledge, swung her legs around, and hopped into the kitchen.

She stuck her head back out of the house. "Easy peasy!" A

second later, she was back on the sidewalk. "Let's see you try."

I sighed. It wasn't about my feet, I wanted to explain. It wasn't about what I could or couldn't do with my body. It was about Dad. It was about Bebe Jacobs, the black leotards, the final selection list without my name on it, the baked chicken with spinach, the empty bag of chocolates, the scale in the bathroom, the number on that scale, the look on Mom's face when she saw that number—all that awful stuff rolled into a cement ball that lodged in my belly. My feet turned to bricks and my legs turned to quivering columns of spaghetti.

"Up you go," Archie urged. "Let's see them tippy-toes."

"Okay," I said. I counted in my head. *One. Two. Three.* I rose an inch. Then another inch. A quiver moved through the arches of my feet. My heels started to shake, and then my calves. The arches of my feet sickled, buckling inward when they should have pushed out. My arms flapped like the wings of a silly bird, and I fell, toppling to the sidewalk, landing hard on my knees. This was the worst I'd ever been.

"See?" I said. "I can't do it."

"Rubbish. Get up," she said.

"Why?"

"Just get up."

She spun me around to face down the street, toward the old church. "See that chuff-off massive tree at the end of the road? Just in front of the church?"

Sunlight threaded itself through the branches of the giant oak. "Yeah."

"What would happen if I ran over and gave that tree a shove?"

"Um . . . nothing."

"Nothing. Right. And why's that?"

"Because it has roots."

"Exactly. It's got roots digging down, deep into the earth. And what are its branches doing?" she asked.

"Growing upward."

"They're reaching for the sky. Growing up to the sun."

"I guess."

"But they couldn't do that if they weren't rooted to the earth, could they? And they couldn't reach up if their trunk wasn't solid and strong." She turned to me and put her hands on my shoulders. "You need to be that tree. When you do your tiptoe wots-it, you need to bear down into the earth, like you're sending roots down into it, all tangled up with the soil and the grass and the mushrooms. And you've got to remember your trunk." She patted my belly. "You've got muscles in there and you know how to use them. Your trunk and your roots are what keep you from falling."

"I want to try!" Jeevan jumped to his feet and joined me, peering at the tree, closing his eyes, wobbling and stumbling.

"And while you're digging down into the earth, you've got to grow upward, too. Your fingertips are those topper-most leaves up there. Reach those fingertips up to the sky, the sun, the moon. Let them sway in the wind, like there's nothing—*nothing*—that could ever bring you down."

Without thinking, I reached out and hugged Archie. She hugged me back. "All right, Lightning," she whispered into my hair. "Let's see what you can do."

So, I began. I closed my eyes and imagined tree roots curling from the balls of my feet and down into the ground, branching out, forming networks that braided into other roots from other trees that passed by foxholes and mole holes, through weeds and rocks and soil.

My heels began to rise. My hands rose from my sides, circling up by my ears in a perfect fifth position. I rose from the balls of my feet, higher and higher, until the weight of my body moved to my toes. I felt my fingers reaching up, up, up to the sky. I imagined pointe shoes on my feet, with their tough, protective casing around the toes. I was doing it! I was almost there! And then I saw Madame Fontaine peering at my feet over the top of her glasses. My toes started to tremble. My heels flew out from under me. My feet crashed to the ground, and the rest of me followed.

Archie sighed. "Well, you made a dog's dinner of that, didn't you?"

I stared at my useless feet. "You had *one job*," I whispered to them. "*One job.*"

She grabbed my hand and pulled me up. "We'll try again later," she said.

Before long, the day started to dim. A field of clouds rolled over Thumpton. The night smelled like rain. We stayed out on

Jeevan's front step until a bank of clouds moved in and blocked the sun completely, until the house's door opened. Paati stood above us. "Dinnertime, troublemakers," was all she said.

When Paati was out of earshot, I turned to Archie. "You're staying, right?"

"How'd you mean?" she asked, the words curling around a yawn.

"I mean you won't run away again. Right?"

Her eyes snapped up to meet mine. "No, I won't run away. I'll have one more barely tolerable year here, and then it's uni and I'll be free. But until then, I'm sticking around. All right?"

"All right," I said. I couldn't help but smile.

"Come on, then, Lightning," Archie said, "let's go home."

TRACK 30
Time After Time

Paati's kitchen filled with the smells of onion and garlic and spices that pinched my nose and made my mouth water. On the stove sat a big pot of chicken curry, and on the table sat a bowl of rice, a bowl of green beans, and a platter of crispy papadums. We filled all four seats around that table, and nobody talked about Archie running away, and nobody talked about the impromptu dance party that had broken out on Alphabet Street. We didn't need to talk about it. We'd all been there. We all knew—without having to say it out loud—that something had changed in Thumpton-on-Soar, that dour and sour little town. Something had sweetened. The tiniest, greenest blade of hope had pushed through the cold cobblestones. Something new had begun.

And here's what I thought about: kitchen tables. Mine, at home, with Dad's empty chair, with talk and laughter elbowing in from next door. I looked around Jeevan's table, filled with food, filled, at last, with the three people who were meant to sit here. That evening, Paati's kitchen was filled with light and chatter and warm, heady smells. This kitchen was nothing like the kitchen that had swirled around me in that first time tunnel. I thought back to those images—Jeevan sitting alone at the table, his schoolbooks spread around him. Paati sitting alone at the table, picking at a plate of food. Archie pushing her chair back from the table and letting it fall with a bang, before zooming in a whirlwind of hair and fury out of the room, out of the house. In all those images, the family had been separated. But here they were now, together.

And here's what else I thought about: going home. How? When? Would Mom be back, or was she still whooping and leaping like a lunatic around London? Would she be sitting alone at the kitchen table, eating with a silent Paati, the shadows sighing and muttering around her? Would she wonder where I was? I felt a sudden pull in my chest—a feeling I couldn't name. Sadness, but not quite. Regret, but not exactly. And then, all at once, I knew. I missed Mom. I missed her with my whole body. I'd been so busy missing Dad that I hadn't noticed it—the aching hole in my chest that could only be filled by her.

Just then, Archie said something to Jeevan, and he laughed so hard he had to spit his milk back into his glass. Paati slapped his hand lightly, but a smile twitched on her lips, too. Maybe this was my mission, to bring these three back together, to make them a family again.

♪ ♫ ♪

After dinner, I helped Paati dry the dishes. Her eyes darted sharply as she worked, and her hands were brisk and sure. She hummed a tune just under her breath. I remembered the crack of her stick on wood. I remembered how she'd danced that day. She sparked like fire in this world of hers. Back in my world, she was more of a mist. But I missed that Paati, too. I missed her mist.

She glanced over at me. "You're more helpful than my children," she said with a curt smile. "Whoever you are."

"You'll know who I am," I said. "I promise." She turned to me then, a little bewildered. Before she could ask me another question, I threw my arms around her shoulders and hugged her sideways. She froze for a second, then picked up a tea towel and wiped her wet hands, all the while watching my reflection in the kitchen window. Her eyes moved from her own face to mine. Hesitantly, she picked up her hand and placed it over mine. Her palm was still damp. Her shoulder was warm and soft. The fabric of her sweater scraped faintly at my cheek.

Dishes done, I found Jeevan in his room, tinkering half-heartedly with the dial on his boombox. He switched from one radio station to another, hardly listening to what was playing. "Nothing good on," he muttered.

I sat down next to him. "I think I'll be going soon," I said.

He scoffed. He hunched over the machine and didn't look at me. "Highly doubtful. You'll probably still be here in the morning, eating my Ricicles."

"I don't know. Maybe."

He wiped quickly at his cheek, which was damp. "How'd you even know you're going?"

"I feel it, sort of, in the pit of my stomach."

"That could be Mum's cooking."

"I don't belong here, Jeevan—"

"Jimmy."

"Jimmy. I don't belong here. This isn't my world. It's not even my decade."

He didn't answer, just turned and turned the radio dial, the static between stations forming its own sort of drumbeat. That's when Archie burst in.

"Ready to try those tippy-toes again, Lightning?"

"Get out!" Jeevan picked up a cassette tape and threw it at Archie. It hit her in the arm.

"Oy! What's got into you?"

Jeevan's show of anger avalanched into tears. They spilled freely down his face now. "She's leaving, Archie. She's going to leave and you don't even care!"

"Well, chuffin' heck, Jeev-o. Course she is. Would you stick around Thumpton-on-sodding-Soar for the rest of your life if *you* lived in California?"

I spoke up. "I would." I turned to Jeevan. "I would, Jeevan. Jimmy. I just—"

"You can't. I know." He drew a long, shuddering breath and let it out. "Well, get on with it, then. Do whatever it is you do. Pool of light, flash-boom, and all that."

On the boombox, a radio station came in, sharp as ice.

222

The notes of an organ climbed through the room, followed by a man's high and clear voice.

"This is Queen," I said. "You should record this one. You'll be happy you did."

He gestured at the boombox. "You know what to do."

I pressed the play and record buttons together, and the tape kicked into its slow march, printing the song onto its memory.

I thought about what it would mean to leave, to go back to my life, to ballet, to no ballet, to Mom and Paati and the last few weeks of summer.

"Could you come back?" Jeevan asked. "Just to visit sometimes?"

"I don't know," I said. "But you'll see me again, no matter what. That much I know." What I wasn't telling myself—what I *couldn't* tell myself—was that Jeevan would see me again, but I wouldn't see him. Not ever.

As he looked up at me, his curly hair sticking up at wacky angles, the light bouncing off his glasses, I saw a sudden flash of Dad. I dropped to the floor and flung my arms around him, and this time he didn't tell me to get off him. He hugged me back, loosely, like he'd been caught by surprise. He couldn't possibly know how much I would miss him.

I could feel the flash coming this time. It was buzzing around my toes, moving to my heels and up my legs. I was feeling lighter and brighter with every passing second, like I could lift out of this life, this decade, and fly.

"I want to try something," I said. "One more time." I

wanted Archie to see me go on pointe. I knew, with the light coursing through me, lifting me up, that I could do it.

"Let's see it, Lightning," Archie said.

I took a deep breath and steadied myself on the carpet. I closed my eyes and imagined roots curling from my feet, down into the ground. And then I felt my heels lift, the familiar clamp in my calves. I pushed against the floor and my heels rose higher and higher, higher than they'd ever gone. And that's when I remembered Dad. I remembered how he'd take me to the playground when I was a kid, his hands tying my shoes for me, his arms pushing me to the sky on a swing. Dad was my tangle of roots—a force beneath my feet, invisible but there. Always there. I raised my arms above my head. I thought of Mom, and I reached up for her, like I had when I was a baby. I could feel her fingers lacing through mine, helping me bourrée and jeté before I could even walk, helping me reach for the sky. And then I thought of Paati, the core of me, strong and solid, there every day, as quiet and still as the trunk of a tree. My thighs flexed and turned solid. Before I knew it, I was on the uppermost pads of my toes. I didn't waver. I didn't fall. I opened my eyes.

Beneath me, Jeevan's bedroom floor was filling with light. My feet started to tingle. The Queen song got louder, its guitar whining and wailing through the quiet room. Archie and Jeevan had backed into the doorway. They just stood there, watching me. The light seeped to the doorway and stopped before it reached their feet. I focused on Jeevan. I tried to memorize his face, to keep it with me forever. Jeevan took Archie's hand and they waved to me. Then, as the light took hold, they froze. It was the last I'd see of them, the picture of them I'd remember forever: a boy with his sister, his lips slightly parted, his hand lifted to wave goodbye. I like to think that they could see me, too: a girl on pointe, bathed in blinding light, her arms reaching for the sky.

All I could hear was the rush of light around me. "Smell you later," I called. A flash. A boom. Goodbye, Jeevan. Good-bye.

TRACK 31
Who Wants to Live Forever

I **woke up halfway under** my bed, with no idea how I'd gotten there. Next to me, the Queen song from Jeevan's boombox was playing on mine. I hadn't pressed play, but there it was, the wheels turning the tape, the last, long notes fading away. The song ended perfectly—no bridge to another song, no DJ's voice, no commercial.

From outside, I heard the shouts of children crossing the street to the park. I heard the hiss of a bus passing by. I was home. And then, I started to remember. The final flash, Jeevan waving goodbye, a slow and quiet fall through the time tunnel.

I sat up and looked around. The house was strangely quiet. A sinking dread started to pool in my chest. What if I'd changed something big about my life? What if this wasn't my house? What if I walked out of my room and found another family sitting at the kitchen table? What if Mom wasn't my mom? What if Dad—the thought flapped around me like a panicked bird—what if Dad was somehow still alive? I jumped up and ran out into the kitchen.

I stopped. My stomach sank. On the mantel sat the green box. I walked over to it and took it off the shelf. Maybe it held something else now, like playing cards or seashells or—or—

"Excuse me, young lady, what do you think you're doing?"

It was Rosario, with Paati trailing behind her. "That's your father in there, you know. Put him back on the shelf where he belongs."

"Sorry," I said. I could feel her eyes on me as I returned to my room.

I'm trying to make you understand how I felt that afternoon, returning to my house, my life, my year. It was kind of like stepping from the shallow end straight into the deep end of a pool with nowhere to stand, no wall to cling to. I was just trying to stay above water, trying to understand my old world, whether anything I'd done had made a dent in it. If I hadn't changed a thing, if this world was just the same, then why did I flash back through time in the first place?

That's when it dawned on me.

What if my flashback had never happened? What if it had all been a crazy fever dream? What if *I* had Covid and fell unconscious and had the wackiest, realest hallucination ever? From the office, Mom's cello tripped happily up a scale and down. Nothing seemed strange. How could I have flashed back through time and not affected a single bit of my life?

I thought about asking Mom, but no. What if I'd imagined it all? She'd think I was going crazy. I would be going crazy. I had to find out for myself. I had to try to go back again. I had to play the tape.

I pulled the boombox from under my bed. Was I ready? Ready for the flash and the boom? I closed my eyes, had a moment with the Big Burrito. *This better make sense*, I said to Him. I'm still convinced the Big Burrito is a man.

I pressed play.

This time, I didn't hear any music, but I did hear a strange clicking sound, like something had turned on. And then I heard a quiet hush, almost like . . . like breath. Like someone breathing. How was that possible? I picked up the boombox and pressed my ear to its speaker. I strained to listen past the static, past the years of gunk that had built up on this tape, and yes. It was the sound of someone breathing.

"Hey, you."

I shrieked and dropped the boombox.

It was Dad. Not Jeevan. Dad. "I reckon you didn't know boomboxes could record voices, too." My heart pinballed around my chest and rattled up into my throat. I could hardly breathe.

"If you're listening to this, Boomi, then you've already been on quite an adventure. I still don't know how it all happened. But listen, you shouldn't go back there again, to 1986. I can't explain time travel, but as a doctor, I can tell you that it probably isn't very good for your health. So that's enough, okay?"

He cleared his throat, then coughed. "If you think about it scientifically, time travel is absolutely, one hundred percent impossible. But there you were. That was you, right? In Thumpton-on-Soar, England, 1986? That was you who pushed my scary big sister off the canal bridge? That was you who saved Archie from running away? That was you who got my entire neighborhood dancing on the cobblestones?"

There was a long silence. Too long. The message might have ended.

"I thought I knew . . ." He was back! I put my palm to the boombox speaker, just to feel the vibrations of his voice. "I thought I knew how the universe worked. Us doctors, we think of ourselves as scientists. We tend to only believe what we can explain. But how could I explain the girl who flew into my life, like a comet, that day in July? You proved that I don't know as much as I think I do. But more importantly, you showed me that there was more to the universe than my little corner of it. More than Alphabet Street. More than Thumpton. More than quiet. More than rules. You taught me that the world was bigger and stranger and more full of possibilities than I had ever imagined. You saved me, Booms. You gave me hope. That's the greatest gift anyone can give to anyone."

Another long silence followed. "I don't know how much time is left on this tape, but I do have some questions for you." He took a long breath. "So, tell me. Would you rather sweat glitter or sneeze rainbows?" And he went on, listing more *would you rathers* than I could count. Each one was a surprise, a gift. When had he thought these up?

"Would you rather soar like an eagle or swim like a fish?

"Would you rather be able to speak any language or travel anywhere in the world?

"Would you rather be a wizard or a witch?

"Would you rather walk on your elbows or sit on your head?

"Would you rather feed everyone in the world or make them laugh?

"Would you rather be immortal or a genius?

"Would you rather have an extra finger or an extra toe?

"Would you rather live on an African savannah or in a Brazilian rain forest?

"Would you rather meet a leprechaun or a genie?

"Would you rather talk to an elephant or—" He went quiet. A short silence. And the tape clicked off.

I pressed play but the tape clicked off again. "What happened?" I asked aloud. I rewound the tape a few seconds and played it again. But it clicked off at the exact same spot. It had run out. "No! Come on!" I whacked the side of the boombox, rewound again and again. Each time, Dad's voice vanished at the exact same moment. I started to wheeze with panic. I picked up the yellow, grimy boombox and shouted into it. "Dad! Come back!" I was yelling now and shaking the thing so hard the tape rattled inside. "You didn't finish! Come back! You didn't get to finish!"

That's how Mom found me: on my bedroom floor,

shouting into the old boombox. She stood in my doorway and stared down at me. I looked up at her and burst into tears. She bounded into the room and sank to the floor and wrapped her arms around me. She wrapped her legs around my legs. She pulled me into her chest and let me cry into the bright, silken folds of her dress. When I felt her shaking against me, I saw that she was crying, too, right along with me. We sat like that for a long time. She rocked me in her arms. Somehow, her small body fit all the way around mine. For the first time in a long time, I felt safe.

TRACK 32
Only You

That night, I found Mom in the kitchen. I felt raw all over, like my body had turned inside out and back again. She'd just gone to the store and was putting the last of the groceries away.

"Hey there," she said. She was watching me carefully, I could tell. She went to the pantry and pulled out a box. "I'm going to have some cereal. Want some?"

"It's nine at night, Mom."

"It's Apple Jacks."

"I'll take some Apple Jacks." I didn't ask her why she'd bought more Apple Jacks, why she was letting me eat an unnecessary and unhealthy late-night snack. And she didn't ask me about the boombox or the mix tape. She didn't say anything about 1986 or London or the fact that she'd traveled four decades into the past.

We sat together, crunching on our cereal, not saying a word, until I couldn't take it anymore.

"Mom."

"Yes, love?"

"What did you do that day? In London?"

She smiled into her cereal bowl.

"I had a glorious time."

"You did?"

"Let's see. First, I went to a bookshop. I had a sandwich at the sandwich place I used to go to during university."

"Wait—how'd you buy a sandwich?"

"I always keep a tenner with me."

"You do?"

"Stop interrupting. After the sandwich, I took a long walk from Waterloo to Hyde Park. It got a bit nippy out so I went into a tea shop and had a cuppa with a slice of Victoria sponge."

"Was it good?"

"What, the tea or the cake?"

"Both."

"The tea was . . ." She trailed off, thinking again. "The tea was heavenly." She went quiet. When I looked up at her, she had tears in her eyes.

"What's wrong?" I asked.

"Nothing's wrong. That cup of tea. It tasted like . . . I don't know . . . like nothing else. Maybe it was the milk they used. Maybe it was the cup. Maybe it was the feel of a hot cup of tea after a long walk on a cool summer's morning. Whatever it was, it was a taste I'd forgotten."

"Like if I went back to Boba Dreams in fifty years."

She smiled sadly. "Sometimes you miss something so badly

that you forget how badly you miss it. And then you find it again. . . ."

"I think I know how that feels," I said. I looked out the window. "Was the cake good?"

She scrunched up her face. "A little on the dry side. We'll make some soon, and you'll see what a Victoria sponge is like."

"Really?"

She raised her eyebrows at me.

"What about losing weight?" I pointed to the Apple Jacks box. "What about your kitchen clean-out? And my audition?"

She nodded, tapping a finger on the counter, thinking. "You've a lot going on, Boomi. You're dealing with . . . a lot." She stared into her cereal bowl. "I was so focused on ballet, I think, because it was something wonderful in your life. I was terrified you'd lose it. And then what? You'd be left with online schooling and a grandmother who's barely here, and . . . you know . . . *me*." She looked up at me then, and something in my heart went quivery.

"Rubbish," I said.

"Rubbish?"

"I like Paati just like she is. And—" I stopped. It was hard to say this. Why was it so hard to say this? Mom's eyes widened, waiting for me to speak. I took a deep breath in. "I like you, too." I let out a big whoosh of air and put my forehead on the table.

"Well," Mom said, "I like you, too."

The table was nice and cool on my head, so I kept it there. "So I don't have to audition for ballet?"

"Oh, you're doing that audition, my friend."

"That's what I thought."

"But you're doing it because you deserve a chance. I want Madame Fontaine to see what you can do. Right now. Exactly as you are. I want her to really see you, Boomi."

I lifted my head. We were quiet for a while. Then I said, "Mom?"

"Yes?"

"What's Paati's first name?"

"Reyvati."

"Reyvati," I repeated. It sounded important, like the name of a mother tiger.

"You didn't know her name? Seriously?"

"Guess who never told me?"

She scoffed and got up to turn the kettle on. My eyes fell on the picture of Dad and Archie that hung on the wall.

"Mom?"

"Yes?"

"I need to ask you something."

She pulled two mugs from the cupboard. "What is it, Pickle?"

"We never used to talk about what happened to Archie. But now I know—she ran away and Dad and Paati barely ever heard from her again. And Paati stopped talking. And Dad lost his sister. But no one ever told me that, you know?"

She dropped two tea bags in their mugs. "I know," she said quietly.

"I had to time travel four decades to find that out. Can we not do that? Can we just talk about stuff from now on?"

She turned to me. "Of course we can. We should have done that from the very start."

"Can we talk about Dad?"

She walked over to where I was sitting and smoothed my hair down behind my ear. "Always. Let's always talk about Dad."

"Okay," I said. "But maybe not always. I mean, we can talk about other things, too."

"Agreed." We just stayed like that for a minute, both of us thinking about Dad, I guess, both of us waiting for the other to start talking.

TRACK 33
Dancing on the Ceiling

Would you rather live on the moon or see it every night from your window? I was looking out at the bright globe of the almost-full moon when Mom knocked on my door. I expected her to burst in, but she didn't. She waited. I didn't answer. I guess I wanted to see how long she'd wait. She knocked again.

"Boomi?"

"Come in," I said.

Mom walked in with a package in her hand. I frowned. "More diet stuff?"

She didn't take the bait. She just placed the bundle in my hand. It was both solid and soft, wrapped in pink tissue paper. Carefully, I unraveled the tissue. The last layer of it fell away to reveal a pair of brand-new pointe shoes. They were made of brown satin, which shone softly in the light of my room. Their satin bands were wide and smooth. I'd never seen anything so beautiful.

"I love them."

"I thought you would," Mom said. "But no pressure, Boomi. You can wear your old ones if they're more comfortable—"

"I want these," I said. "Can we break them in?"

"I'll get the hammer." When Mom left to get the hammer, I brought the shoes to my lips. "I'm going to dance in you," I whispered. "You're going to be my roots and my trunk and my leaves." The shoes said nothing, just glowed softly in the light.

That night, Mom and I hammered and bent and stretched my shoes. She sewed an extra ridge onto the toe pad. Ballet dancers do all kinds of crazy things to make their pointe shoes easier to dance in. They shave off bits of the sole, they scrape the soles with a blade, they pack them with extra padding, they hammer them down to flatten out the toes. I wouldn't be surprised if they set them on fire, just a little. Even after they're broken in, they'll still hurt. Before long, the satin will scuff away at the toes. There's no getting around that. What you see on stage looks like magic, but behind that magic is a nonstop punch-out with reality.

Speaking of reality, there was one detail Mom was overlooking. My little trip through time hadn't changed a thing in my world—that included my body. Even if Archie flashed forward from 1986 and personally kept me on my toes, that wouldn't have changed one important fact: I had the same body. If it wasn't a ballet body then, it wasn't one now, either.

Lying in bed, I couldn't sleep. The shadows slumped into their corners, bored. I pulled out the junk box and found the old handkerchief. *RG*. Reyvati Gopalan. I ran my fingers over the embroidered letters, lumpy and uneven, like scar tissue on the white fabric. They weren't pretty, not like the perfect little flower on the other corner. The *RG* was crooked, rough. I wondered if this handkerchief was sold at market, with Paati's clumsy little initials sewn in. Maybe the factory didn't know about these initials. Maybe they were Paati's own quiet rebellion, her way of saying *I am here.* I folded up the cloth and tucked it under my pillow. A cavernous yawn took hold of me, and before I could even finish it, I was asleep.

Just after dawn, I woke up to a jolt, like a truck had slammed into the building. I shot up in bed. The jolt came again and again. The room shook. My books jiggled on their shelf. Our house creaked and clattered and swayed. An earthquake!

"Mom!" I called. A second later, she burst through my door and grabbed me out of bed. We stood in the doorway, holding on to the wall, as my books tumbled to the floor and my water glass tipped over. A few seconds later, the shaking stopped. Mom and I looked at each other. I could feel her heart pounding against my arm.

"I think that's it," she said. "I'll go check on Paati."

I checked my room for any damage. I'd been through little earthquakes before, but never one that big. Under my bed, the boombox had toppled over. Outside my window, the street was quiet and empty. The sun was starting to rise.

Mom and I found Paati sitting up in bed, her hair spilling

over her shoulders. I sat next to her, picked up her hairbrush, and started working it through her long, tangled locks. Mom brought her tea. Mom brought Paati tea every morning. Every evening, she heated milk for her, sprinkled with cardamom and saffron and brown sugar. Paati had lost Archie, but she'd gained Mom. I sat with Paati for a long time, neither of us saying a word. When sunlight filled her window, I kissed her soft, papery cheek, and left.

TRACK 34
Your Wildest Dreams

Here's the thing about life returning to normal: It becomes totally, completely normal. No flashing away, no time tunnels, no creepy churches or Disco Baba or buses to London. The long afternoons are as long as ever, the boring bits just as boring. That first afternoon back in my house, I was gathering up the books that had fallen from my bookcase, wedging them back onto their shelves, when my door opened. In walked Bebe.

"Hey," she said, and flopped right down on my bed. Normal.

"Hey," I answered warily. We sat like that, saying nothing, in total silence for exactly one eternity, when she finally spoke up. "Your mom said you have an audition tomorrow. Are you ready?"

"No," I said.

"Are you going to do your audition piece, or something else?"

241

"I don't know."

"Have you practiced?"

"Not really."

"Well, what have you been doing?"

I scowled at her. "I've been doing a lot, Bebe. Just not practicing my dumb petit allegro." I thought about it. I didn't want to do that audition piece, anyway. It made me think of that disastrous afternoon, just days ago. It felt like months. I sighed. "Why'd you come here anyway? I thought you'd be hanging out with Cece."

She rolled her eyes at me. "Jealous much?" Yes, actually. Jealous much. Jealous a lot. "I came over to get boba. It's Thursday afternoon, remember?"

"What?"

"Thursday afternoon." She looked at me like my brain was leaking out my ear. "You know what happens Thursday afternoon, right?"

"Um, *yeah*." Um, no. Nothing happened Thursday afternoons. Nothing happened ever. What was Bebe talking about? We stared at each other again, neither of us saying a word.

And then, from the silence, the smallest, most distant drumbeat. Bebe's eyes widened. *BOOM-hiss-hiss-BOOM-hiss.* The beat carried up the street, getting louder, getting closer. I cranked my window open and the music sailed in.

"It's here!" Bebe yelped.

"What's here?"

"Disco Boba!" She ran out my door.

Disco Boba. My mind erupted with questions. I'd never heard of Disco Boba, but it was so much like Disco Baba—*what was happening?*

I followed Bebe out the front door, just in time to see a truck clunking and sputtering down our street—a pink truck hung with tinsel and glittery baubles. Across its side, in bubbly green writing: DISCO BOBA. And then: FOR ALL YOUR BUBBLE TEA NEED'S.

My heart *boom-hiss*ed in my chest as the truck sputtered to a stop. We stood at the order window, the first in line. A long line was forming behind us. We waited. Nothing happened.

And then the truck's window slid open. A woman leaned out of it. A sound flew out of me—something between a laugh and a shout and a huge, body-shaking sob.

She saw me and her face exploded into a smile.

"All right, Lightning?"

She was a grown-up now, but her eyes were still lined in black pencil, she still wore fingerless gloves, and she still had her blinding smile. It was Archie. It was completely and totally Archie!

Archie leaned out of the truck window. "First in the queue, as always, eh? What can I get you this fine afternoon?"

Bebe spoke up first. "Hey, Archie Aunty! I'll have a strawberry milk tea with fifty percent sweetness and brown sugar boba, please."

Archie's eyes stuck to me, searching, wondering. Then her gaze flitted to Bebe. "Coming right up, madam." She nodded at me. "The usual for you, Booms?"

I think I must have answered. A minute later, I was holding a cold, frothy milk tea with mango exploding boba and heart jellies. I'm not sure what happened after that, except that Bebe and I walked to the park. I remember seeing the Ferris wheel that towered over the park and walking past the art museum. I remember sitting on a bench while Bebe talked and talked. All I could think about was Archie.

Eventually, Bebe got tired of me not talking and left me standing at my front door. I didn't know if she was mad at me. I didn't care. The boba truck was parked and closed now, but I heard voices coming from inside the house. I ran up our stairs and burst through the front door.

I saw them before they saw me. At the kitchen table sat Mom, Paati, and Archie. Next to Archie was a woman I'd never seen before. Except for Paati, everyone was talking over each other, laughing and calling out, each of them stirring or blowing on or sipping from a cup of tea. When they saw me, they quieted down. For a moment, the house hung in silence. Archie was the first to speak. "We were just talking about this morning. Quite the trembler, wasn't it?"

Mom just sat there, sipping her tea, like it wasn't bonkers that Archie was here. I looked at the woman next to Archie. She had short dark hair colored pink at the tips, and a ring that hung right between her nostrils. She smiled at me like she knew me. Her eyes were a deep, bottomless blue. "Who are you?" I asked. Mom and the woman broke into giggles again. Even Paati smiled a little.

Only Archie stayed serious. She cocked her head to the side and studied me calmly. "Oh, very droll," she said. "Is that any way to greet your Jenny Aunty?" Then Archie reached into her bag. "You're a very rude child, but I've brought you something, because I love you anyway." She slapped a packet of ginger biscuits on the table. I looked at them. I looked at her. She winked at me, then turned back to the table and carried on talking about the earthquake.

Out in the living room, when she was getting ready to leave, Archie pulled me aside. She studied my face, my eyes. "It's happened," she said. "Hasn't it?"

"How—how is this—?" I had a hundred questions that never got asked. Archie pulled me into a big, soft, endless hug. "I don't understand what happened," I said, my face squished into her shoulder. "Mom's acting like everything's normal."

"Well, everything *is* normal, Poppet." After a few seconds, she pulled away so she could see me. "No. You're right. Nothing's normal. Not without him."

I nodded and tried not to cry. I did a bad job.

"I know," she said, smoothing down my hair. "Nothing's normal at all." She studied my face for a few seconds. Then: "I lost my dad when I was ten, you know."

I nodded "So, you know what it's like."

"I do," she said, "and I don't. It's different for everyone. And in some ways, it's the same."

"I'm glad you're here, Archie Aunty."

"So am I." She hugged me for an even longer time. Then she stood up and shrugged on her jacket. "Jenny!" she called. "Let's get a wiggle on!" Jenny hurried from the kitchen, kissed me on the head, and followed Archie out the door. "See you tomorrow, Lightning!"

"Yeah, see ya," I said, pretending to know what she was talking about. Then I remembered: tomorrow. The audition.

Later that afternoon, Mom and Paati watched me put on my ballet shoes. "Sure you don't want your pointe shoes?" Mom asked.

"Not yet." I wanted to get the routine down before I attempted pointe again. And I sure as heck didn't want to go back on pointe with Mom watching.

Mom started the music on her phone, the tinkling piano notes I knew so well I could probably sit down and play them myself. I counted to eight, heaved a sigh, and began.

I knew the routine inside and out. I moved through the steps and nailed every single one. But something was off. I did the routine again, then once more. Finally, I saw it. My dancing was boring, ticking along like a machine. What was it missing?

I tried once more, hitting every sauté, every turn, like a good little robot, and finished with the final notes of the piece.

"Perfect," Mom said. "Beautiful."

I looked for Paati's reaction, but she had none. She sat slumped against the side of the sofa, her eyes closed, her mouth open. A snore roared out of her.

"Paati." Mom tapped her arm. "Paati, wake up! Boomi's dancing for you!"

"It's okay," I said. "I don't blame her. It's putting me to sleep, too."

Mom raised her fist to her forehead and blew out hard— she was trying to be patient. "Well, that's your audition piece, Boomi," she said. "You *have* nothing else."

"But maybe I do."

"Oh, you do, do you?"

"I do." I didn't. But I wasn't going to trot onto Madame Fontaine's stage and lumber through that three-minute yawn of a dance. She probably wasn't going to let me in anyway, right? So why not do a dance I really loved? There had to be something I could do. There had to be—

Batteries. From nowhere, Denny's shout popped into my head. *Batteries.* I couldn't get the word to leave me. *Batteries, batteries, batteries.*

"I'm going to go work on it now," I said. I had no idea what to do, but I had that word: *batteries.* What did batteries have? Power. Charge. New energy.

247

Paati let out another glorious snore that woke her up. She looked straight at me. "Nattadavu number five, please," she said drowsily, then closed her eyes and went back to sleep.

In my room, I did the combination Paati had asked for. It felt good to thwack my soles on the ground, to stretch my fingers, to bend in ways ballet never asked for. It felt as good as a sauté or a glissade.

Next, I danced a révérence, the ballet version of Paati's Namaskaram. I bowed to my imaginary teacher, to my imaginary pianist. The pointe shoes soaked up the lamplight, their soft sheen melting into my skin, brown on brown, until they looked like they'd always been a part of me. I swept my arms wide to thank the top tiers of the auditorium, to thank the boombox, the universe, and the Big Burrito. My imaginary audience leaped to its feet and cheered.

And that's when I knew. Ballet wasn't my enemy. Madame Fontaine may have been pushing me out, but ballet wasn't. I loved it. My body loved it. And sometimes, even when it was really hard, ballet loved me. When I unlaced my shoes, my feet ached in a familiar, comforting way. And that's when an idea started to grow, small and shy at the back of my mind. The more I thought about it, the braver it grew, until it crept from its corner and stood, small but proud, at center stage.

"I know what I'm going to do," I said to the shadows.

I expected a rush of dark around me, the shadows gathering around and waiting eagerly for more. But when I looked for them, they were nowhere.

I opened my laptop and messaged Bebe.

Me: Hi.

Bebecakes6471: What was wrong with you today? You were being weird.

Me: I need you to meet me at my house. I have a brilliant idea.

Bebecakes6471: This better be good.

An hour later, Bebe showed up at my door. I told her my brilliant idea. She stayed for dinner. It's like we were friends again. We *were* friends again. This time, the neighbors' voices and laughter on the other side of our wall didn't seem so loud.

That night, with plans for the next day's audition spinning through my head, I fell asleep. And that's when it happened. I can't explain it, except to say that I wasn't scared or confused. It was strange, sure, but somehow it all made sense. As I slept, I started to see things. First, I saw Dad in the kitchen, pulling steaming strands of spaghetti from a pot, Archie Aunty pinching a strand to test how cooked it was. Mom stood close by, tearing basil leaves. Jenny Aunty grated parmesan into a bowl. Paati was there, too, sitting at the kitchen table next to a big bowl of salad. Somehow, I was sitting right next to her. The side of her mouth tweaked into a sly little smile. She plucked a cherry tomato from the bowl and popped it into my mouth. I could feel the tomato skin break between my teeth, the burst of sour juice, the tickle of tiny seeds on my tongue.

More memories came: Archie holding out a pair of pink leg warmers. Paati telling me a bedtime story, her hand resting placidly on mine. Christmas morning, the grown-ups gathered on the sofa, Dad on the floor with me, sorting presents into separate piles. A family trip to India, Mom buying me a Cadbury bar at the airport. Paati, her hair still black, slapping her hairbrush into her palm and singing an old Tamil song, croaky and out of tune. Archie and Dad arguing about something in the living room, and Archie slamming the door. Archie coming back a few minutes later, looking sheepish, and hugging Dad around the shoulders.

All night long, the scenes spilled into my head, a big messy pile of them.

When I woke up the next morning, I remembered them all. It wasn't like a dream that you half forget the second you open your eyes. These weren't dreams at all. They were memories. They had *happened* to me. Together, they made a life—a life full of people coursing through our house, of family and laughter and fights and meals. Somehow, having Archie around had changed my parents. They'd become less quiet, less lonely. I didn't have to wish for the laughter and talk from the house next door. In my new life, we were the noisy ones.

I wondered what the shadows would think. I looked around, waited for their hushed questions, their unhelpful comments. I checked the corners of my room, the floor by my bed, my closet, the hallway. I couldn't find them. Not a single shadow anywhere. When did I last see them? I could hardly remember.

That's when I realized: Archie Aunty had stepped into my life and scared the shadows away. The house was too loud for them, I guess, too full of people and possibilities. Too full of life. "Smell you later, Shadows," I said aloud. Nobody answered. They were definitely, totally gone. Did I miss them? Not one bit.

My sweatshirt lay at the foot of the bed. I fished inside it and pulled out Dad's note. *You can change your life.* That's just what I had done. I had changed my life.

TRACK 35
Don't Stop Me Now

The next afternoon, Bebe found me backstage. I was wrapping tape around my toes, getting them ready to jam into my pointe shoes. She handed me my toe pads. "Are you ready?" she asked. "Do you have that transition combo down?"

Before I could answer, Archie Aunty came up right behind her. "Give 'em hell, Lightning!"

"I will," I promised.

With my shoes laced up and ready to go, I peeked out at the audience.

At the official audition, we had a piano player. Today, all I had was a cell phone and a speaker. And that's just how I wanted it.

I walked out on stage. It was bigger than I remembered. The ceilings of the auditorium were higher than they'd ever been. The vast field of empty seats stared back at me. Toward the rear, in the middle of a row, sat Mom. Archie Aunty and Paati sat on either side of her. Mom had wanted to leave Paati at home, but I wanted her there. Madame Fontaine sat in the front row, clipboard in hand, the overhead lights beaming off her giant glasses. She looked bored.

I looked down at my feet. *You'd better work*, I said to them. *Please.* I nodded to Bebe. She pressed play. A jolt from above, and I was bathed in the warm tunnel of a spotlight.

A moment of silence, and then a man's voice sailed through the dark, trailed by the clear, climbing notes of a piano:

Tonight, I'm gonna have myself a real good time. . . .

Dad's favorite Queen song. I moved into fifth position. Plié, soubresaut, glissade. I felt good on my feet. Dance had taken hold, but I hadn't gone on pointe yet.

A few beats later, it was time.

I closed my eyes, imagined the big tree at the end of Alphabet Street, its roots digging into the ground. The little gears in my feet and legs sprang into action, and my heels started to lift. My calf muscles burned. I thought of the trunk of the tree and my quadriceps kicked in. My stomach muscles wrapped around me like armor. I reached my arms up, up into the sky. I thought of the spray of green at the top of that tree, sunlight winking through its leaves. My toes pushed up into a full pointe. This was where I always fell. This was where my middle always started to quiver, where my ankles usually turned to jelly.

I didn't quiver. No jelly. I looked out at Mom. She looked back at me. Her face was as calm, as steady as that old tree. And me? I was officially, totally, completely on pointe.

I did it!

And I stayed upright, reaching for the sun, rooted to the ground. In bourrée, with its dainty little steps, I traveled across the stage and ended, at last, in a fifth position plié. I had done it. I had done it! I wanted to stop everything, throw my fists in the air, and cheer.

But was I finished?

Not even close. The music played on.

Through the dark, I caught sight of Paati. She wasn't asleep this time. Her eyes bored into mine like lasers, like the dance teacher with the wood block and stick. Paati looked like she knew exactly where she was and exactly what I was going to do.

The music's tempo picked up. My heart raced. I put my hands to my waist and stamped my foot. Madame Fontaine jumped in her seat. I stamped my other foot, then launched into every Bharatanatyam combination I had ever learned. Madame stared up at me. She wasn't bored now. I jumped and stamped across the stage. I moved from Bharatanatyam to ballet and back again. Whatever I'd choreographed, I forgot completely. My plans flew out the auditorium door, and I just danced. Angry goddess, lightning bolt, a deer in the woods, a hunter! Pas de bourrée, fouetté, grand jeté! Renegade! Chicken Noodle Soup!

Madame Fontaine stared at me, her mouth hanging open, her hands clutching her armrests. Farther back, Mom sat with her hands over her mouth, her eyes wide. I couldn't tell if she was smiling or crying or both. Archie Aunty bopped in her seat, her fists pumping in the air.

The music got faster, and so did I. The music reached a fever pitch as my body stormed across the stage. I was every type of dance. I was everything, everyone, everywhere. I was there. I was there. I was there.

The music slowed again, the guitars faded off, and all that remained were the chords of a piano. I finished in fifth position, my arms at rest. The singer's solitary voice, pure as diamonds, echoed into silence.

Archie Aunty jumped to her feet and whooped. The rest of the auditorium was perfectly quiet. "That's my girl, Lightning!" Archie Aunty called. From backstage, Bebe ran out and threw her arms around me. She leaped and whooped around the empty stage, ran circles around me. I caught Paati's eye, and I'm almost positive she laughed. Madame Fontaine just sat there, her face as blank as a slice of bread. I could see Mom watching Madame Fontaine from behind, waiting for a reaction. But Madame had been stunned into stillness. Only her glasses moved, sliding down her nose, and falling, at last, into her lap.

Very slowly, Mom rose to her feet and started to clap. When Archie Aunty stopped cheering and took her seat, when Bebe quieted down and left the stage, Mom kept going. I just stood there, listening to the solitary clap, clap, clap of her hands. I knew that as long as I kept standing there, the spotlight bearing down on me, she would keep clapping. I have a feeling that if I'd never walked off stage, we'd still be there today, in that auditorium, looking out at each other, her hands sending me their brave and lonely beat.

TRACK 36
The Whole of the Moon

I got rejected again from the Academie Fontaine. Shocker.

I am ballet, I am Bharatanatyam, I am Renegade and Chicken Noodle Soup. But I am not, it turns out, Academie Fontaine material. It's okay. I pretty much knew that. Mom wanted Madame Fontaine to really see me. One thing I knew for sure was that Madame Fontaine saw me. She couldn't have missed me if she tried.

The important thing is, Mom didn't cry or plead or stomp down to the director's office when we got the rejection. Instead, she sat me down at the kitchen table.

"You still want to do ballet?" she asked.

"Can I?"

"Of course you can. There are plenty of dance schools around. And I'll bet none of them have seen an angry goddess."

"But the Academie Fontaine is the best school in the city."

"Says who?"

"Says Madame Fontaine."

"I want you to think about that for a moment."

I did.

Mom sat down next to me. "Is it the dance school you love, or is it the dance?"

"It's the dance."

"Then you'll keep dancing."

"Really?"

"For as long as you want to."

I couldn't imagine ever not wanting to dance. Mom cupped my chin in her hand, gazed at me for a few seconds, then got up to make dinner.

"I heard she puts on the accent," Mom said.

"What?"

"Madame Fontaine. She isn't French. She's from Florida. Her real name's Mimi Finkbeiner."

"Really?"

Mom giggled quietly to herself as she rummaged through the fridge. I guess we're all just figuring out who we are—even Mimi Finkbeiner. We're all auditioning for something.

After dinner, I pulled the boombox out from under my bed. I thought about rewinding Dad's mix tape, pressing play, and seeing if I could flash back to Thumpton-on-Soar. I could relive that all again. But why? Sure, I missed Dad. But Jeevan wasn't exactly Dad. Dad wasn't Dad until he had me. I missed Jeevan, too. But I guess it's okay to miss people. It means we love them, and that's not a terrible thing, is it?

Outside my window, I heard Denny howling at the moon. It was full and bright in the sky. That's when I knew what to do.

I pulled the tape out of its compartment and shut it safely in the junk box. Then I carried the boombox down to Denny.

"I think you should have this back," I said.

"But it's your dad's. Don't you want it?"

"I'll loan it to you. I think you should try it out."

"For real?" he asked.

"Totally."

"Well, let me give you something for it." He started to dig in his bag.

"It's okay, Denny."

Denny pulled out a Rubik's Cube. "For you," he said.

"Thanks." I handed him the boombox, and this time he accepted it. He peered into the tape compartment and blew imaginary dust from the buttons. "Do you have any tapes?" I asked.

"Do I have tapes? Do *I* have *tapes*?" He dove into his sack again and pulled out a plastic bag bursting with old cassette tapes. He spilled the bag out on the ground, got down on his knees, and sifted through the pile. "I got the Stones. I got Hendrix. I got Joplin. I got Otis. Gotta love Otis, right?" He picked one out and held it up to me. "I got a bootleg of a Dead show from '72 that Jerry Garcia *himself* was trying to get his hands on." I didn't really know what Denny was talking about, but one thing was clear. Denny had tapes.

"Choose carefully, Denny," I said. And then I explained to him, step by step, how the boombox worked. He nodded along, like I was showing him how to work a blender.

"Got it."

"Are you sure?"

"Sure as sugar."

"Okay, well, have fun." I didn't know how Denny's flashback would work. What if he flashed away and never came back again? "When you flash away, Denny, I'm gonna take the boombox back. You can have it whenever you want it."

"Roger that."

"Have fun, I guess."

Denny gave me an elbow bump and ruffled my hair. "You keep booming, Boomi-girl."

"I will."

I watched from my window upstairs. Denny put on his giant rucksack, ready for his voyage. He crouched by the boombox, pressed play, and huddled down, watching the tape turn, waiting for something to happen. From where I stood, I heard a few faint strains of a guitar.

The ground beneath his feet began to glow. The light spread outward, streaming down the sidewalk, pooling in the gutter. The night grew brighter and brighter, until it was bright as day. "Here it comes," Denny called. He stood up straight. "Here it comes! Yeeeeeeaaaahhh, baby!" He froze with his arms in the air. The street flooded with golden light.

A flash. A boom.

When I looked down, Denny was gone. I wondered what he would find on the other side of that time tunnel. I wondered if I'd ever get to know.

Later that evening, Mom brought me another present: a brand-new boombox and a pack of blank cassette tapes. Boomboxes and tapes still existed, I guess. I could start making my own radio mixes. I still had the old boombox, but I decided to put it away. At least for now.

Here's another thing Mom did. She decided I should start "talking to someone." That meant I had to go to a therapist. It's not as horrible as it sounds. I didn't have to lie on a sofa. She didn't ask me weird questions. She just let me talk, and sometimes she talked back. Here's something she told me, which I think is pretty true: You don't just lose someone once. I lose Dad every day. Every time I wake up and he isn't there. Every time I want to tell him something and can't.

But here's what I came up with: If I lose him every day, then I keep him every day, too. I keep all the trips to Boba Dreams. I keep his box of junk. I keep the stories he told me, the games we played. And I keep his music.

The first thing I did with my new boombox was to put Dad's mix tape into it. I didn't know what would happen—whether pressing play would flash me back to the past again. I knew I wasn't supposed to do that anymore, but I couldn't help it if it happened, could I? I held my breath and hit play.

The first chords of the first song started. I squeezed my eyes shut and waited for a flash, a boom. But nothing happened. The first song finished playing, then melted into a few seconds of a DJ talking, before it cut off. Then the second song played. Then the third. Sometimes, I'd hear little snippets of radio commercials from 1986, for things like chewing gum and furniture shops. It was just another mix tape.

Listening to it, I thought less about Dad and more about Jeevan. I thought about that summer day I landed in his life. I thought about the brand-new boombox, bright yellow and perfectly clean, and Jeevan babbling on and on about mix tapes. But here's something he didn't mention. Life is a lot like a radio mix, and the people you meet—they're the songs. You keep them or you let them go. Some songs you like right away. Others have to grow on you. Some songs are good to dance to. Others you save for quiet, lonely afternoons. Not every song has a clean beginning. Some get cut off early. But the point is, you never know what song you're going to hear on the radio. When a song that you love comes on, you feel incredibly lucky. You run to the boombox and hit record and you thank the Big Burrito that you were there that day, that minute, to hear it.

Acknowledgments

I want to first acknowledge the tens of thousands of healthcare workers who lost their lives during the Covid-19 pandemic, whose dedication to helping others meant they kept going to work, while many of us got to stay home. Their children and families live every day with their sacrifice.

In researching my book, I discovered creators whose work inspired mine, among them the *Three Pounds in My Pocket* podcast, Dawinder Bansal's *Jambo Cinema* art installation, and Rajeev Balasubramanyam's "George Michael and Me."

My heartfelt thanks go to the many people who shared their experiences and knowledge with me: Rani Sanghera and Rajeev Balasubramanyam, who shared their memories of growing up Asian in eighties Britain; Jyoti Argade, for talking to me about Bharatanatyam; and Rasika Misri, for talking Bharatanatyam, ballet, and letting me try on her pointe shoes; Spencer Dutton and Grahame Foreman, for sharing all things eighties music and eighties candy; my parents and brothers, but especially Anand Sekaran, for gently correcting my medical scenes; my writing group, Laleh Khadivi, Mūthoni Kiarie, Keenan Norris, and Joel Tomfohr, for their encouragement and feedback; Holly Roberson and John Goldstein, for giving me a space to write; the Bus Stop Betties, for bringing me coffee and snacks as I worked toward deadlines; the Berkeley Ballet Theater, for bringing ballet to the people; and most important, my two boys, Avi and Ash, for their love, their healthy skepticism, and for keeping me on my toes.